BLACK HAT
JACK

BLACK HAT
JACK

 The True Life
Adventures of
Deadwood Dick,
as told by
His Ownself

JOE R. LANSDALE

Subterranean Press 2014

First Edition

Limited Edition ISBN
978-1-59606-676-2

Trade Hardcover Edition ISBN
978-1-59606-677-9

Subterranean Press
PO Box 190106
Burton, MI 48519

subterraneanpress.com

For Turon Tanner

BLACK HAT JACK and me had been riding at night, trying to take in the cooler weather, avoid the sunlight, but mostly avoid being seen. That was almost queered when Jack said he smelled Comanche. I had known Jack a while now, and I had learned that when he said he could smell a bear, a buffalo, a Comanche, or a ground hog fart, then he most likely could.

We got down off our horses, bit their ears and pulled at their necks and they lay down for us. It was a pretty bright night, and that fretted me some, I assure you. Them horses, some fairly tall grass, and tumble weed and some Texas dirt, was about all that was between us and them. I took off my hat and tossed it aside so as to get smaller.

They wasn't right on us, maybe twenty-five feet away, and we could see them good, crossing in the moonlight.

Must have been twenty of them. More than enough to ride down on us and lose a few, but still take us and do what they like to do to them that cross their lands. Story was they ran the Apache pretty much out of Texas, and let me tell you, if there's someone that can run an Apache, you best take heed of them.

So there we was lying down behind them horses, our teeth clamped on a horse ear, which is not tasty at all, though horses themselves are pretty good to eat if you cook them right. The horse I had on the ground was a fellow I called Satan. He wasn't the original horse I called Satan, as I had to eat him, (which is what made me an expert on the eating of horse) but this one was pretty good, black as the one I had before, and about of the same spirit, though less mischievous. He would even come when I whistled. If he was in the mood.

I'm tempted to tell you a story or two about the original Satan, but I suppose what you want to hear about is the Comanche and what happened to us. Since I'm here telling you about it, and I'm not going to talk about Satan the First, I guess there's no use telling the old joke about the frontiersman who sat down with some tenderfoots and told them about the time he got out on the trail and was surrounded by twenty Indians at each of the four directions, mean and nasty and angry and well-armed. But I'm going to tell it anyway.

They was coming down on him in a rush, and all he had was a pistol with six shots in it. He'd tell the story like that, warming it up like he was tossing a log on the fire, saying what them Indians was wearing, talking about the scalps flapping from where they hung on their horses, or on spears or such, and then he'd say how he fired all six shots, and knew he wasn't going to have time to reload. He'd pause in his story then, stop and light his pipe, or scratch his balls, or some such, and wait for the inevitable question.

"What happened?" a tenderfoot would ask.

To which the frontiersman, leaning forward in earnest, stretching out the moment, would say, "Why I got kilt, of course."

Only this night wasn't no joke. I was seeing if I could smell them Indians, but I couldn't. All I could smell was wet horse ear. I kept my teeth clamped on it without biting so hard the horse got angry and started tossing its head and trying to stand up, just firm like to suggest it might be a good idea if it laid still. Some people taught dogs to do that, jump up and grab a horse by the nose or the ear, and bring him down. That was quite a jump, but we wasn't dogs and this wasn't a joke. Them was real live Comanche braves.

We lay there quiet and watched them ride by, wrapped in buffalo robes, scalps dangling from their bridles. Those robes were a little heavy for the June weather during the day, but at night it could get a shade nippy. I had on my heavy coat for that matter, and so did Jack, though mine was woolen and his was buckskin lined with wool. Jack also had on a hat made of buffalo hide that had fold down ear flaps. It was black as the devil's shadow and he always wore it, snow or shine, and that's how he got his name. He had been a mountain man and was now a hunter and sometime scout for the army, but though he looked the part, with beaded moccasins and such, he was always good about his grooming. He got rid of lice and fleas promptly in both hair and beard, and would bathe and soap up, wearing his red flannel long handles as he did. He liked to keep those clean too.

After the Comanche had gone on, we still laid there and didn't move. It was like we had been planted in that ground and was just waiting for a rain so we, as seeds, could burst up out of the ground, mounted and ready to ride.

After a time, Black Hat Jack let go of his horse's ear, and that horse stood right up, and Jack swung into the saddle. I did the same. We started trotting slowly in the direction we had been going, which wasn't the direction them Comanches was heading.

"That was close," I said.

"Comanches riding in a group like that are out to raid, and this is a good night for it. I got no idea where they're going, but they got plans, or hopes, or maybe they're just traveling like us. Sometimes a Comanche can seem to be doing one thing and he's doing another. In other words, I know some shit about Comanche, but I don't know all the shit there is to know about them. No one does. Not even the Comanche themselves."

I, of course, knew all this, as I wasn't exactly attending my first goat roping. I had been all about the business of Indians before, but it was good to have Jack with me. He was a man you'd want at your back you got in a fight. He even treated me good, and him a white man. Or at least whiter than me. My figure was he was some Indian, and probably some Irish or Swede, and a whole lot of horse's ass. He was a hulk, had somewhat dark skin and those hard, sharp features of an Indian. I don't even know what his last name was. I'd never asked. I always called him Jack, and some called him Black Hat Jack, and time has washed his name from history a bit, as I tell this, but there was a time when he was as well known as Liver Eat'n Johnson, Kit Carson, Jim Bridger, and Buffalo Bill. Well, maybe not as much as Buffalo Bill.

Wasn't nobody as well known as he was, except maybe Wild Bill Hickok. I had known Wild Bill some and could appreciate that he wasn't all legend and no sand. Actually, same could be said of all them I mentioned, though Buffalo Bill was the least shy among us about lying and maybe the one with the largest hole in his bag of sand, cause he used lying for more than just entertainment. He made a living out of bragging, and it made me a little jealous.

Lying was something you was supposed to do up to a point. It was the sign of a real frontiersman, someone who had been around. And I have learned myself how to do it, and I have gotten my lessons from the best, like Black Hat Jack. He could lie like a preacher, and look as sincere as a politician wanting your vote, a banker wanting your dollar, or a whore that has just told you how fine you was, even if you was the twelfth in line that day.

But at the core of it Jack was honest. Stood up for his friends, and he was a straight shot when it come to a rifle, though not as good as me with pistols, and a straight shooter with words when he wasn't yarning, and maybe as good as me there. I do stretch the truth a little, though I want to assure you I ain't doing that now. This is all the truth as it happened without any stretching of facts, though some of the facts are a little hard to remember, and therefore have to be filled in some. I don't consider a fill a stretch.

Another thing about Jack, wasn't no one knew how old he was. He carried himself like he might be forty at the top, but his wrinkled face, his thin, gray hair, marked him up at about sixty or more. That said, I never heard him complain about hard or cold ground or bad weather or shitty food, though there was one exception as he made quite a point to me that he wouldn't eat mash potatoes unless he was held down and they was shoved down his throat. I don't know what he had against mash potatoes, but the feelings didn't extend to the tater in its truer form, as he would eat those raw, or baked for that matter, certainly fried up in buffalo grease, or lard or butter, but the mash potato had somewhere along the line hurt his feelings, and he hadn't never gotten over it.

We was riding along after our close call, and then we seen something lying out on the ground. It was like a mound of light-colored dirt with sticks in it, but that wasn't what it was. When we got up on it we seen it was a man. He was naked and stretched out, tied down. It was clear the Comanche had been at him. They had probably started on him during the daylight and had worked on him most of the day. Stakes were driven in the ground at his hands and feet, and his arms and legs had been stretched out and tied off to them with rawhide. They had fastened a rawhide band around his balls, and when it shrunk the balls swelled up and burst open. Black Jack said they had used wet rawhide and let the sun dry it. I had once been wrapped up in a fresh killed cow skin, wetted down and left to dry, and not by no Indians. I had barely escaped that one, but I

hadn't gotten out of that hide before the sunlight tightened it and I began to feel it squashing me like a mouse between two bricks. I was lucky that day. Some folks I knew come up on me and cut me out of it.

This fellow, he hadn't been so lucky. He had been worked over elsewhere too, had his eyes poked out and something stuck up his nose, and his mouth was wide open and full of dried blood, which my guess was from having his tongue cut out. His beard had been skinned in spots, and trips of skin had been peeled from the top of his chest all the way down to his groin. His stomach had been cut open and his guts was pulled out and placed on a fire that was burned out now and was nothing but blackened sticks. Those guts was still attached to him; they had cooked them while he was still alive, and on top of it all he had been scalped. Like I said, you didn't want to get caught out there in the wild with the Comanche, and that's the reason so many frontiersmen saved the last bullet for themselves, or for someone they cared about.

It's hard to imagine such things sitting in your house all comfortable, and the frontier having been cleared out a few years back, but that's how it was back then, and that's how you would do if you were smart; you'd use your last bullet for yourself.

"It's a buffalo hunter, I bet you," Jack said. "Comanche don't like them especially, killing off all their food for the hides. They wouldn't like them much better if they took the meat, but seeing that meat rotting out there, just the hides and maybe the tongues taken away, it sets a Comanche's teeth on edge. I ain't fond of it neither."

"Ain't we hired out to hunt buffalo?" I said.

"We are, but I'm not proud of it. Billy Dixon, who's the one told me about these herds out near Adobe Walls, said he hated doing it, but it was either leave them be and be proud of yourself, or make a dollar, and the dollar won. That cleared things up with him, but I got to tell you, more of them I've killed, more I think about it, it's getting a lot more murky to me. I ain't got nothing against them Indians, none of them, though I will admit to being less fond of the Comanche than others, but they're just doing what they need to do to survive."

"Ain't that what we're doing?"

"Reckon so, but I don't feel noble about it. Dollars I make doing this, well, son, they don't shine. I think I am one of a whole pack of worthless son-of-a-bitches, and though I like you and find you better than most, you have to be included. All us humans are fouled on both ends. One we shit out of, and the other we talk shit out of. If god was fair about things, he would have already smashed the shit out of all of us. I know I'm full of it, and I suspect you are. Thing is, just when I think I'm done with it from either end, I fill up with it all over again."

That's how Jack was. He was going to die a philosopher, not a Christian.

We didn't have a shovel, but we used our knives to dig a grave, taking turns in case we got too deep in our work, so to speak, and not see something creeping up on us, like an Indian. The ground was hard, but we got a grave dug that could hold that dead man down under. Parts of him we found in the grass, skin and the like, we put that in there with him.

When he was packed away, wearing a coat of dirt, we got back on our horses and rode on. I had never been to Adobe Walls, which was our destination, in the north top of Texas. We was to meet up with Billy Dixon and the others Jack knew. Jack had been there before, and knew the way. Once he'd been to a place he claimed he could always go back. I was a pretty good tracker, and wasn't bad with direction, but I was beat out by a lot of others, and especially Jack. I figured you could have blindfolded him, ridden him on a horse over the Rockies, pushed him off his horse and broke his leg, and somehow he'd known the direction to crawl to get back to you and cut your throat, and he would never have to take off the blindfold.

2

WE COME TO Adobe Walls after another day, late in the afternoon, and it wasn't much. It was some adobe walls, as its name suggested, and they was falling down, and there was one dirt street, if you could call it that, a blacksmith shop and a store, and a hole of a room with broad doors that Jack said was a saloon. All of this was surrounded by wagons, stacks of hides, plank-walled outhouses, and out a piece beyond this ruined encampment was deep buffalo wallows where those critters had rolled about tossing dust onto their hides to fight the fleas, which on a buffalo, as well as their hunters, could be considerable. Some attempt had been paid to put up some high posts for fortification, making a kind of wall of them. But the builder had gotten lazy and had quit the job, so there was plenty of open spaces. It really wasn't much protection against man nor beast.

There was a rise beyond the place, about a mile away, and there was a couple of creeks, one thick with trees of all sorts on either side of it, if you can call a West Texas tree a tree. Back where I'm from, East Texas, we call them bushes. Once Kit Carson had fought some Comanches at this place, and on the prairie near about, and got his ass handed to him, though it was called a victory by the whites and he got all kinds of commendation for it. That's the way whites worked. You slaughtered an Indian, it was a victory. They slaughtered you, it was a massacre. In this case it was mostly Kit and his men running and the Comanche chasing.

There was horses tied, and there was some grass bundled for them, for a fee, and there was grain for a bigger fee. This was all handled by the blacksmith who looked too small to shoe a horse, but he made up for that by being skinny and having a small head.

We settled in our horses and unsaddled them, got them paid up, and Jack carrying his Sharps and me my Winchester, our pistols on us, we headed into the saloon, which was next to a store we passed. Store's doors was wide open, and its shelves was visible and there was stuff on them, but all I remember seeing was cans of peaches. When we come inside the saloon it was near dark, or seemed that way at first after us being out in the strong sunlight, and the stink of all them buffalo hunters and skinners met us as we come in and gave us a greeting we wouldn't never forget. Every stinking underarm, crotch, every lice-infested head with greasy hair that had gathered up buffalo blood, every un-wiped butt, burp, fart, and assorted smells that could stick the pages of a book together, was there to say howdy. I tell you, I almost swooned, and it being dark to the eyes was making it worse, because it was like some kind of rotten giant was standing over us and we couldn't see him.

Then the cracks of light that shone through the gaps in the walls and through the windows, which had greasy oil cloth pulled down mostly over them, was clearer and seemed to grow because our eyes had gotten used to things, and we could see who was in there.

There was a bunch of men standing or sitting about in rough-built chairs, and they was festooned with pistols and knives. Rows of Sharps rifles in all calibers you could imagine was leaned up against the wall. There was a bar full of splinters from men sticking their knives into it, and it was made of planks and crates and looked as if it might tumble over with a sneeze. The place was held up with poles, and the pole in the middle looked strained and the roof, which was coated with sticks and dirt, appeared ready to tumble down on things. The center pole especially made me nervous as it was bowed a bit.

We was about six feet in when one of the men said, "Hey, now. No niggers in here."

It was a Southern voice, and I seen him moving away from the bar then, pushing his wide-brimmed hat up a tad. He had left a Sharps rifling leaning on the ramshackle bar, but I could see he had a pistol in his belt. I had pistols too. A Colt on my left hip, and a LeMatt revolver on my right. Those LeMatts are pretty well forgotten now, but mine was given to me by a Mr. Loving, who was after my Pa a kind of mentor. It fires nine rounds, and if you thumb a little baffle on the trigger guard, another trigger can be worked, and that fires the under barrel load, which is a 4/10 round. It's for close up work. I was also carrying my Winchester, which has a loop cock and a baffle on it, so I can fire it just by cocking it and closing the lever. It's hard to hit anything that way, but it'll sure cause folks to jump, and if they're close enough you just might put a round through them. I say that because that's how it is with most men. Me, I can hit things with it. If it sounds like I'm bragging, forgive me. But it's true. I can shoot a shot up a gnat's ass and knock out its teeth, make them line up like piano keys in front of the little bastard's corpse.

That's a bit of an exaggeration, I admit. Gnats don't have teeth.

The man was swaggering toward me. I said, "Hello to you too, you goddamn peckerwood, shit-eating bastard."

Well now, that caused the air to thin. The other men was silent for a moment, and then a young one laughed out loud, a fellow that was probably no more than a teenager, maybe twenty if you gave him an edge, but walked and talked like a grown man. The young one said, "He knows you, Jimmy," and then the others laughed.

When the laughter died down Jack bowed up and went into a kind of monologue that caused him to sway, way a spreading adder snake will stand on its tail and swing its body above the grass, flaring its head to look scary. "You all know me, the one and only goddamn Black Hat Jack, called such on account of my hat is black and my name is Jack. Nat, standing right here black as the Ace of Spades, is my partner, and due to his shooting prowess in Deadwood, is also known as Deadwood Dick. Paint on the skin don't matter. You lift a hand to him, I will kill you and skin you and pack you with buffalo shit, and kick you till you are alive and can stand. Then I will kill you again, and if I've got the need, I will fuck your corpse. Is that understood, you bunch of ignorant, buffalo hunting, dog-fucking, shit-sucking, dick-kissing, ass licking excuses for grown men that ain't even dropped your balls or got hair above your peckers?"

These words hung in the air along with the stink for a while, and then the young man stepped forward, said, "Well, I think that pretty well names us, and there is plenty of buffalo shit out there, and I for one don't want to be skinned, and the thought of Jack's pecker in my ass is enough to frighten me off most anything. Hello, Nat. Step up to the bar and I'll buy your black ass one."

With that everyone laughed, including the Southerner, and he said, "Damn right. You're a friend of Jack's, you're a friend of mine, and your black skin is just as white to me as any white man's."

"Thanks," I said. "That is damn white of you."

"That's my take," he said.

There was more laughing, and me and Jack stepped up to the bar, and a jug came out and the young man who had lightened the mood, who I could now see was dressed as dapper as if he was going to a ball somewhere, his mustache waxed and his hair greased and parted down the middle, said, "Let's knock them back."

His clothes looked clean and he smelled pretty enough to live in France, or some place where the light was bright, the water was pure, and the children and women didn't ever fart.

He stuck out his hand to me, said, "Bat Masterson."

I shook his hand.

"Glad to meet you," I said. "I'm glad you had you a sense of humor."

"It has served me well. Sometimes, when nothing is going my way, I tell myself jokes. It lightens the mood. Let's have a jug, barkeep."

The cup set in front of me looked like it had been used to dip that buffalo shit Jack was talking about, but when the whisky was poured, I lifted it to my lips. Now, you got to understand I never was a man to drink liquor or beer. I always preferred sarsaparilla, which often got me some laughs and some kidding, but considering the circumstances of where I was and who I was with, and the way things had started, I thought it best to suck me a cup and seem sociable. I did that from time to time, though I can't say I ever built me a taste for whisky, and this horror from the jug was worse than anything I had ever put in my mouth. Only thing I could come close to thinking it reminded me of was once, when I didn't have no place to sleep, I slipped under a porch in Abilene and was awakened by a yellow cur pissing on my face, and right into my open mouth. This wasn't quite that tasty, but it was similar.

"What the hell is this?" Jack said, having downed a cup himself. Remember, I told you Jack wasn't a complainer, so this should give you some idea of the rankness of this libation.

"Well," Bat said. "They call it whisky, but it's only a touch of that. It is boiled with snake heads and a squirt of horse piss and some twists of already chewed tobacco by men without teeth."

"Oh, don't tell me that." I said. "You're kidding."

"Nope, he's not," another man said.

I turned to that fellow. He was a tall man with dark hair, a little beard and mustache. Like Bat, he was dressed pretty snappy as far as his type of clothes was concerned, but it was a snappy that had gone dusty and dirty, and he had the smell of skinned buffalo about him.

"Say he ain't?" I said to him.

"He isn't lying," the man said. "I only take a snort of this when I have to, and right now, I have to. Set me up, bartender, and don't hold the horses. To the lip and don't get a match near it."

A cup was poured for the man, and he pushed up between Masterson and myself, said, "By the way, I'm Billy Dixon."

"I know of you through Jack," I said.

Billy turned and looked at Jack. "Why, me and Jack have shared many a buffalo wallow and the fine roof of trees and sky, and we once shared a whore who was so fat you had to take survival supplies and a detailed map with you just to get around her ass."

Billy turned to Jack. "To Fat Ass Willamena, as good a screw as a pretty girl. And I wish she was here right now."

They drank to that, lifting their cups first in a toast, then downing the contents with one mighty gulp. Me, I didn't drink with them, just pretended to, touching the rim of the cup to my lips and putting it down.

WE WAS STANDING there in that strained light, and
in comes a woman and a man, and Jack, who had
taken to the far end of the bar next to Bat, leans
beyond him to me, says, "That there is Mrs. Olds and her
husband. She ain't available. They run the store."

He said this as if I was planning on asking her for a
dance and a possible visit to a hay pile later. She wasn't
much to look at, thick and big-boned, and though I
wouldn't call her ugly, she was as plain as homemade
soap with a wad of hair in it. My take was she could
have used a bar of it on herself, with or without the hair,
and not just because it was a rough living out where we
was. When she come up to the bar with her husband,
she said, "Give me the straight stuff, and wipe out the
goddamn cup first, and not with your fingers."

Her cup would be the cleanest thing about her. She was six feet from me, and had a smell that was whupping the hell out of that that was already nesting in the room, the one collected from all them men. It was the kind of smell that doesn't come from a sweaty afternoon, but from years of not washing unless she was caught in a rain, and I was certain if she was, she'd run from it to shelter as fast as she could. If she had been available to me, I wouldn't have wanted to venture what kind of stink was under them dark, dirty skirts she wore. She was about the nastiest looking and smelling thing I had ever seen, and considering some company I'd kept, that was some kind of thing to say.

Mrs. Olds downed her cup of poison, yelled out, "Oh good goddamn, that is the shit, there. God-a-mighty, piss up a rope."

Her husband, a stout man with a hound dog face and maybe three strands of hair on his head, had quietly ordered his cup, and now he sipped at it, looked at her as if hoping she might ask for another cup and that a fresh drought of it might strangle her. She did have another, but she didn't strangle. That was when she looked down the bar and her eyes having adjusted good, settled them on me and said, "Is that a nigger?"

"Yes, m'am, I suppose I am." It wasn't any use trying to fight being called that. It wasn't worth the stirring.

"Well, how the hell are you?" she said.

"Fine," I said. "How are you?"

"I got a twitch between my legs, and my old man here has a razor strop for a dick. Loose and floppy, but not as long. A good sized cigar laid next to it would make it look like the nub of a near used-up pencil."

"That is more knowledge than we all need," Bat said. "Charlie, I think your wife might be deep in her cups."

"I ain't had but them two," she said.

"Here," Charlie said. "But you drank a jug-full at the store."

She rocked her head back like that sort of talk was revolting, said, "Well, goddamn you, trying to tell me how to drink and how much of it, and keeping up with it like you're measuring out milk for biscuits. Mind your own dick-jerking business."

She pulled a knife from somewhere then, a slit in her dress, I think. It wasn't long, but in the weak light from outside it shimmered a little and made me believe it was sharp. To Charlie, she said, "I'll cut you from ball-sack to eyeballs, you needle-peckered excuse for a grown man."

Charlie had his right arm on the bar, and he kind of heaved his shoulder and his fist came up and hit her solid on the jaw, knocking her backwards against Jack, who caught her. The knife fell on the floor.

Charlie slipped in then and got his arms around her and hoisted her up like a sack of potatoes over his shoulder. "The lady's sleepy," the weight of her bowing his legs.

Normally, striking a woman wouldn't have settled right with me, but for the first and only time in my life it seemed like a good choice had been made, and my guess was that was to her the same as a goodnight kiss.

Charlie opened the door, carried her out, and slammed it shut.

Billy said, "She cut him up a little not long ago. When she sobered up, she stitched him with a needle and gut-string, kissed him and told him what a lover he was. Next day when he was able to stand, she got drunk again, got into with him over something or another, ripping out his stitches. She told him after that if she ever acted up, just to slug her. I don't think she meant it, but he took her at her word, I see."

"I think someone asks something of you nicely," Jack said, "you should be ripe for doing it."

"I have to agree with that," Bat said.

Several other men had leant an ear to the conversation, and they agreed that a good punch in the mouth if asked for should be delivered, be it man or woman, horse or dog. Jack backed off on the dog part. He could see the others, but a dog he wouldn't buy into. Dogs were all right with Jack.

I don't guess I have to mention that this was a particularly rough crowd.

WHAT WAS LEFT of the day was getting a sack thrown over it, and what light there had been through the windows and the windy cracks in the boards where there wasn't anymore. Lanterns was lit.

"I figured I'd let it lay until we was kind of drunk, as that's how I take things better," Jack said. "But me and Nat here, we seen some Comanche, and then we seen what they had been at. A fellow who was cut up and burned and scalped. Had a black beard. Wasn't much to tell about his face, as he was knifed-up good. Color of eyes was two dark holes, and so was the nose. Can any of you put some hair to that, some nose and eyes? He was missing his johnson too."

"Was he tall?" said Jimmy, the man who asked if I was a nigger when we first come in.

"I don't know he was so tall," Jack said. "Do you, Nat?"

"Not as tall as me," I said. "Maybe tall as you. He had a big belly, but that may have been because they cut him open and his guts was pushed out."

"That will swell you," Billy said. "Being dead swells you, but guts right out there in the open in the sunlight, even if the air's cold, it'll swell a fellow. Everything gets bloated in size. A small man can look like a carnival wrestler. I've seen it."

"Where was the body?" Jimmy asked.

"Up near Chicken Creek," Jack said.

"I'm going to guess it's Hutchinson," said Jimmy. "That's the direction he took, and he ain't come back. He and his partner went for a hunt on their own, even though we didn't think there was no use in it. We all felt the herd hadn't come far enough this way yet. Let them come to you, is what I say. You get so you can tell how they're going to do."

"Only way you can tell," Billy said, "is if someone tells you they're coming or the buffalo show up and stand on your feet. The rest of us can tell, but you can't tell your ass from a hole in the ground."

"The hole is below me, the ass is behind me," said Jimmy.

"Goddamn, he's gotten smart," the barkeep said.

"His partner," Jimmy said. "I figure they got him too, or otherwise he'd be snugged up here with the rest of us, out of the cold. He wasn't one for more hardship than he had to endure. Hutchinson, he might could take it, but that partner of his... What was his name?"

Nobody knew.

"Whatever it was," Jimmy said, "I didn't never call him that twice, as I didn't care for him. I think he liked his hand in his pocket more than he liked a woman, way he talked. All that said, I guess ain't nobody deserves that, being cut up by them savages like they was a link of sausage for breakfast."

"Them savages ain't no worse than us," Jack said. "They ain't ones to keep their word any better than us cause they know ours isn't any good, but they got a streak of honor about them, mean as they are. You might could ask Nat here about savages. His color and his kind have seen plenty of that, and they were white-skins. As far as them redskins go, this is where their people lived before we knew there was a dirt beyond the ocean. Someone come to take land we owned, we'd buck too."

"Ain't like they're doing anything with it," Jimmy said.

"Who says they got to?" Jack said. "And what have you ever done for this country other than slaughter buffalo and shit in the bushes?"

"You do the same," Jimmy said.

"I do," Jack said, "and that's why I say ain't none of us worth a flying fuck in a snow storm. Fill up my goddamn cup again. Let's lift one to poor old Hutchinson and that other dead fellow we don't know the name of. May Hutchinson stay buried, and may that nameless son-of-a-bitch be somewhere alive, and if dead, may the wolves eat his bones and may their shit grow green-green grass." That was the toast, and I actually sipped a bit more, but just a bit. As I put my cup down, Jack turned to it, and knowing my ways, took mine and drained the remains.

There was more toasts and more cups poured, me having turned mine over so as to show I was done, and as the night went on the voices got louder. There was jokes and lies told, and some things that might have been the truth. A man in a bowler hat said how he could throw his bowler hat and make it fit on anyone's head. The barkeep volunteered as victim, as he was hatless, and Bowler Hat, whose real name was Zeke, I discovered, cocked that bowler with careful aim, one eye squinted, and away it sailed. We watched it travel across those darkish quarters, and hit the barkeep in the face, banging his eye. Well, then the fight was on. Bets was placed quick as possible, but it wasn't quick enough. Zeke took a beating so fast, he hit the ground before his knocked-out teeth. Afterward the barkeep punched his fists through Zeke's hat, so that rain and sunshine would be the same to the top of Zeke's head.

We all decided this was just too mean, and we all chipped in and Jimmy went next door to the store, and come back with a new hat, not a bowler, but a wide-brimmed one the color of wet dirt, and tossed it on Zeke's chest. He then told us he was happy to report that Mrs. Olds was sleeping peacefully in the middle of the floor, her head on a flour-sack, one eye swollen shut. Mr. Olds was watching her carefully, knowing she would finally come awake. He was living in fear of the natural born fact that he had to sleep sometime, or so said Jimmy, though as I have reported, all of us was something of exaggerators.

⑤

FTER A FEW pukings and passing-outs, things began to wind down considerable, and there was only a few more shenanigans, among them a cuss-fight, which was seeing who could string the most cuss words together and have it make some kind of sense. Jack won. Well, there was a peach-eating contest. Some fat blowhard said he wished he had some peaches, and that he could eat his weight in them, to which Bat replied, "I judge you about two hundred and ten, and they got canned peaches next door."

"Well," said the blowhard. "Maybe not my weight."

"Let me see you eat twenty-five cans of peaches, and I will give you twenty-five dollars," Bat said.

"That's a lot of money," said the blowhard.

"You fail, you give me twenty-five dollars, or that spare Hawken rifle you got."

"What the hell you want that for," some fellow said to Bat. "Now that they got a Sharps, them Hawkins ain't the gun you need."

"Call me a fucking historian," Bat said.

So it got called that there would be a peach-eating contest, and somebody went next door to the store and bought the peaches with money we all chipped in, and they was opened a can at a time with a pocket knife. Damn if Blowhard, as I had come know him with some affection, take to them without pause, lifting the cans and pouring them peaches and the syrup they was in down his gullet like a wet fish sliding between mossy rocks. About the time he got to the fifteenth can and was looking spry, Bat started to pale. I was wondering if he had twenty-five dollars. On went Blowhard, volunteers opening the cans for him, him lifting them to his lips, gulping them like water, and then when he hit can twenty, he began to shake a little and took to a stool, sat there with the sweats.

This heartened Bat, but there was still some worry, as there was only five cans more.

"I got to pause," said Blowhard. Then he burped real loud, cut a fart that made the nastiest among us ill, and went back at it. He swallowed all twenty-five cans of peaches, took twenty-three dollars and a pocketknife from Bat for the rest, had a whisky, lay on the ground and cried.

More time passed, and by then we was all sagging, especially them that had been about serious nipping. It was decided that we'd hunt in the early morning, so some of the men went to set their skinning wagons and clean their rifles, and make necessary preparations. Me and Jack was shooters on this trip, not skinners, so all we had to do was wait until first light, which was going to come mighty early.

Jack and me decided we'd stretch out on the floor of the saloon, like some of the others. We got our bed rolls and laid them flat. We took off our coats. The night air was no longer cool. It was already growing hot from the oncoming day, though darkness was still about us. We was slipping our pistols and knives off our persons when Blowhard began to roll around on the floor moaning. "Oh, my pancreas. I've busted my pancreas."

Jack hooted. "You goddamn idiot. You wouldn't know where your pancreas was if I cut you open and laid your hand on it. Go to the outhouse, jackass."

Blowhard got up with a lot of effort and went to the outhouse, saying, "I still believe it's my pancreas."

Me and Jack laid our weapons at the sides of our bed rolls, then dropped down on top of them to sleep. I got dunked into a well of slumber mighty fast and deep, and that's why when that loud snapping sound come, I thought I was a ghost already.

Jumping up, grabbing my Winchester, looking around, I saw Jack and a room full of men doing the same. That precarious timber I had mentioned, why it had snapped and the roof was sagging.

"It's got about enough strength to hold a few more minutes if a fly don't light on it," Jack said.

That led to some of the men going outside with the idea to tear down one of the poles that was supposed to be part of the Adobe Walls fortifications, and substitute it for a new support pole. The rest of us took to the roof to pull off some of the sod to lighten the roof, which led to some bad gaps in places. If it rained, a lot of us and a lot of the bar would get wet.

When I was done helping, I went outside. It was still dark, but there was streaks of pink in it like blood poisoning. I looked at that for awhile, then noticed my horse wasn't in the place where I had corralled it. As the blacksmith was up and about, I went over and said, "Where's my horse?"

"It and the others are picketed down by the creek," he said.

"By the creek? Why, that's a good stretch away. Why don't you just offer them to the Indians, and tell them to come back tomorrow for the saddles."

"Now listen here young fellow, you better watch your mouth," he said.

Jack had come up now. He said, "Where's my horse?"

"Picketed at the creek," the blacksmith said.

"The creek?" Jack said. "Why the pig shit would you put him down by the creek? There's Indians about. It's where they live, goddamn it, out there in the nothing, the prairies and the trees. Is your head packed with mud?"

"A horse has got to drink," said the blacksmith.

"Bring the water to them," Jack said. "That's what buckets are for."

"It's a lot of trips," said the blacksmith.

"It is at that," I said. "That's what we're paying for. And besides, you could shorten the trips if you carried the buckets only as far as the well, which is right over there."

"It was just easier to take care of them all in one swoop at the creek," he said.

"But it's still a bad idea," I said.

"What he said," Jack said.

"Oh now, don't give me trouble," said the black-smith. "It's alright. I'll go down there and get them right now if you want them."

"We ain't ready to ride nowhere," Jack said. "But bring them here close, and watch them. Or give us back our money."

"I got a mind to do it," he said.

"Tell you what," I said. "Take out for the grain and such for the horses, and give the rest of the money back. We'll go down to the creek and get our own horses."

"You do that," he said.

"The money," Jack said.

"Now, tell you what," said the blacksmith. "I'll go get them, and I'll keep the money. I'll keep them up here for you, way you like. I'll be so sweet to them they won't want to leave."

Jack looked at me.

I said, "Your call."

"Oh, what the hell," Jack said. "I have by nature a goddamn sweet disposition. Go down there and get them and keep the money."

So away went the blacksmith.

When he was gone, Jack said, "Goddamn stupid ass."

We walked to where the walls was broken down the most, and as the light had cracked the sky good and was falling over things like sunlight was heavy, we looked and seen the blacksmith hustling toward the creek. There was a run of trees along it, and our horses and others was picketed out, like they was an offering to the Comanche.

"It's like he's lived in a tree all his life," Jack said. "He hasn't learned a damn thing. It's a wonder he ain't dead. I think he's the kind of man that will run for politics when he gets the chance."

We watched as our horses was taken off the picket line. The blacksmith had ropes looped over their heads and noses, and he was leading them toward us. That's when he threw up his arms and let go of the horses and made a coughing sound, staggered forward, then began to run. He headed toward us like he had been born on a hill, one leg seeming shorter than the other. But closer he got, we could see something sticking out of the back of his calf, causing him to limp. It was an arrow. Now our horses was loose, the others was there for the Comanche to take, and the dumb blacksmith had an arrow in his leg, which at that moment was the lesser of it to me.

"We got to get them horses," Jack said.

I had left my Winchester inside for the moment, but I had my handguns, and so did Jack, so we broke for the creek like we was running to a party, and in a way, we would be if them Indians got us. They had to be situated down in that creek.

The blacksmith ran right past us, saying, "This way, you fools."

I realized then he might actually be smarter than we were. We kept running though, and when we reached the picket line some arrows whizzed by us like hornets. I pulled my pistols, one in either hand, and started firing toward the creek. I heard a grunt from there, and then we was at the string of horses. Some of the other men from the fortifications, such as they was, had come to do the same, rescue their horses. Bullets barked and arrows whistled. Pretty soon all those horses was free, and we might actually have hit some Indians. I know that grunt I heard sounded serious enough. Here's the thing though. We didn't actually see none of them.

The horses was loose, and we started running them toward the walls, and there was other men there now, trying to run them into the corrals. The only horse that wasn't there was Satan. He had taken to the prairie or was already captured by a Comanche. Jack's horse walked from where he was and went into the corral as if he had just remembered he forgot something there.

We looked up and seen the ridge that was beyond the creek and the trees was filled with mounted Indians. Not ten or twenty, but more of them than you could count with a pencil and paper.

There have been all manner of estimates since the fight at Adobe Walls, and I don't think any of them have nailed the truth to the wall. Some said we was eighteen men and one woman, some we was eighteen counting the woman, and others have said we was twenty-eight. And though I must admit I didn't take a head count and write down everyone's names, I would say to you that we was over thirty, maybe thirty-five.

Problem was there was a lot more Indians. At a guess, I'd say there was at least five hundred of them. I've heard said there was a thousand, which is too much. I've heard two hundred, which is too few. Let's just say there was enough there to give concern. And let me tell you, they was a sight, them redskins. All festooned in war bonnets, or plumes of feathers stuck to the side of their heads. Them that was bare-headed had hair greased out with buffalo fat, and it shined in the sun. They was all half-naked, or full-naked, but for strands of leather around their necks, wrists, waists, and ankles, from which hung ornaments of brass and silver and bright-white bone. Many of them had round shields of wood and folded buffalo hide. Their horses was painted up in all kinds of colors, yellow and reds, and blues, and enough scalps hung from their bridles to supply hair enough for every white man in the state of Texas to have a wig made, and one that would soundly fit them. I just took it in at a glimpse, mind you, as it didn't seem standing still was a good idea, but it was a sight. Majestic and wickedly beautiful, but at the same time enough to make you wet yourself and look for a hole to crawl in.

From the side come running a couple of men waving their arms, one of them yelling, "The wagons, there's dead men in them. They done been snuck on and kilt."

They meant some of the buffalo hunters that had gone to sleep away from the saloon. This all seems mighty odd in the telling, us out there in Comanche country, the blacksmith picketing the horses at a creek, and then them men that going out to sleep in their wagons, away from the main gathering of us, and all of us armed. But that's how it was. All of them, and I have to include myself, had become too confident; the confidence afforded to us not by common sense, but by lust for the dollar.

Another man ran up from behind us and was almost shot by all of us. "They got the peach-eater. He's out in the shitter, they turned it over on him and killed him with his ass hanging out, the sons-of-dog-bitches."

"Get inside the store," Jack yelled. This was like asking a fish to swim or a bird to fly. Men was already swarming for the door, and at the same time them Comanche was whooping and howling and riding down off that hill. As we got to the door, we seen there was Indians on foot that had snuck upon the camp. Truth was, that support pole cracking had got us stirring just in time to discover all them savages. They was starting to surround us.

I was still handling my pistols, and I wheeled and shot one of those Indians that was on foot dead, just as he reached a low point in the wall. I was about to shoot another come from the same direction, a little man with long, dark hair in braids, wearing all white buckskins, or at least they had started out white, when he jerked both hands above his head, started waving them like he was trying to catch humming birds.

"Don't shoot me," he said. "Save me a place inside. Don't shoot my ass. I'm a white man."

It was reckoned, by me at least, that it might be some kind of trick, but that voice was pure Texas, and as he come on closer, bullets darting by him and slamming into the low walls near us, arrows flocking around his head like birds, it was clear he wasn't no Indian. I might also mention that though he run with some vigor, he was a sloppy runner, his elbows flying all over and his arms now flapping at his sides like he was trying to fan a fire out on his ass.

When he got to the wall, however, he proved quite nimble. He come over it with a leap, landed on his feet, and passed me on his way inside the saloon.

Well, here come them Indians then, and I seen then that they wasn't all Comanche. There was Cheyenne out there too, but I didn't stop to make sure I was correct on the matter by checking out their hairdos and such. We rushed inside and closed the door, and hadn't no more than thrown the latch over it, than they was beating on it with fists, bows, lances and rifles. They was hooting and a hollering so loud it was setting my teeth on edge.

Now they was at the windows, breaking them, firing in. They hit somebody, cause I heard him yell out, and when I turned he was on the ground at my feet, having passed his shadow to the other side. That's how close I come to getting elected.

I had a clear path view to the window, because many of the men had dropped to the ground or cuddled up behind something like it was their best friend. I cut down with that loop-cock Winchester, riddling the

frame of the window something furious, knocking out what glass was left, as well as sending lead bees through it. One of them plowed a furrow through an Indian's scalp, dropping him like a bad habit. The others that had been swarming there at the window, even planning on crawling through, was now gone, having decided on another game.

Men was up with their weapons now. The few windows in the place was all on one side of the building, and they was in a flash protected by men with rifles. Thing was, not everyone there was a crack shot or a hunter. There was some that was just skinners, others that was teamsters, and so on. All of them could pull a trigger, but that didn't mean everyone there could hit what they was shooting at.

Jack was at one of the windows, and like the others was firing as fast as he could send a round out there into the air, throw out the casing, and load a fresh one. The Indians was firing back, and bullets was tearing into the walls, and in some places cutting through them like they wasn't no more than bed sheets. I fetched up behind a barrel and got low, knowing a good round might go through a weak spot in the wall, the barrel, my head and whoever might be behind me, and maybe through the other wall and knock off an unsuspecting prairie dog lingering over his breakfast. Those Indians was well armed. They had bows and arrows, some spears, but they had modern shooters too, and when I thought about the number of them up on that hill, the number of us inside the store, I figured we had about as much chance as a block of ice on hot stove.

They was still banging on the doors, and some had crawled on the roof. That was a bad thing for us, as the roof had gaps in it from where we'd peeled off the sod, and the place that had been fixed up there wasn't anything that was going to thrill a professional home builder. We fired up through the ceiling a number of times, heard grunts and yips, and was rewarded by seeing one roll off the roof past the window and hit the ground hard enough a cloud of dust puffed up. Them others lit out of there like their breech cloths was on fire.

After furious shooting at us from outside, none of us was hit solid, though there was minor wounding. Our shooters was claiming to have cleaned the clock of four or five Indians. The men near the windows stayed there, and while they did, the rest of us stacked feed and flour sacks up against the walls, three and four thick. We piled them up to the window bases, so that men could stand at them for protection and see out and pick off targets that presented themselves. I tell you, it was touch and go all the while. But finally we wasn't being set upon like we was before, and the shots fired only came now and then, being most likely snapped off by those who was bored or felt they hadn't gotten their chance.

It was then that we turned our attention to the white Indian. He was squatting behind some flour sacks pushed up against the wall. Questions was being called out to him.

Jack said, "I know you. Ain't you I Got A Hand In My Ass?"

"Hair," the man said. "It's I Got A Hand In My Hair. It's an Indian name."

"No shit," Jimmy said. "We thought maybe your old Mama from New York City called you that."

"My white name is Happy Collins," he said. "I come from a long line of Happy Collins, and I'm not from New York. I'm from Nacogdoches."

"You don't look all that goddamn happy to me," said the barkeep.

"At the moment, I am feeling somewhat dour," he said.

Bat said, "We can see that."

"What in hell are you doing out here without no weapons, running like a school girl from a bunch of Comanche?" Jack said.

"It's not just Comanche," he said. "Cheyenne as well."

"I knew it," I said.

Everyone gave me a look. It had just kind of slipped out. But hell, I did know it.

"There are Kiowa too," he said. "Led by Lone Wolf. And the Cheyenne are led by Big Bow, Little Robert and White Shield. But it's mostly Comanche, and they got none other than Quanah Parker as their leader, and Quenatosavit."

"Translates White Eagle," Jack said.

"Now that there is good to know, and if we just knew all their wives' names, and kids', maybe their favorite horses'," Jimmy said, "we could sleep tight tonight, though our throats might be cut."

"No, it's good to know who's who," Jack said. "I know of all of them names, and it tells us what we're up against."

"We have all been out of the city, Jack," Billy Dixon said. "We know those names as well as you do."

"There's a chief named Little Robert?" Bat said. "I didn't know that."

"That's because you're a kid, still wet behind the ears," Billy Dixon said.

"Well, I'm all up for any man here wants to try and dry them," Bat said.

Bat just got laughs.

"I mean it," he said.

He got more laughs.

That's how them hunters was. They was the sort to laugh when another man would be crying.

"I have lived with the Cheyenne off and on over the years," Happy said. "Until today I got along fine with them. I have a Cheyenne wife, Horse Woman, and she is fine. Or I did have one. I have been taken out of the family, it seems. A divorce."

"And why is that?" I said.

"I have been someone who works both sides of the street for quite some time. I like certain aspects of being white, but the Indians are really good about not making you work, at least in a common way. The women do all the work, and the men sit around and watch them work, hurry them about it, tell stories, go hunting and fighting."

"Sounds like a goddamn paradise," Jimmy said.

"It has its benefits, but Quanah, he's done got the ass itch for the whites, and wants to run them out, and he's got the Cheyenne in on it, some Kiowa, and even though Quanah is half-white himself, he has decided we all have to go. He actually talked White Shield, my father-in-law, into giving me the option of having my nuts cut open and stuffed with hot pebbles, or I could try and run back to the white people and take my chances here. I liked my father-in-law, and am surprised he turned on me like that. Now I may have to go back east and go to work for my father's law firm again. I hated that."

"You might as well had your nuts cut and packed," Jack said. "This here isn't going to end well neither."

"I see that now. You know there's a lot of warriors out there, and they are in a bad mood, and they think they got magic on their side. Or did. There is some dissension now. I heard some bad language exchanged from some non-believers, right before they asked me to leave."

Right then we heard some pounding on the wall from where the outfitter store was, and the adobe began to break, and then the head of a pick-axe come through. Rifles turned in that direction, waiting. The hole got bigger, a face appeared there, but it wasn't an Indian face. It was Mr. Olds, he of the right cross to his wife's head.

"Don't nobody shoot now," he said, "it's me. Doors in here won't hold as good as yours, and there's four of us here, counting my wife. We want to come through."

"Then we got a goddamn hole in the wall to contend with," Jack said.

"It's not like we can run outside and you can let us in. We'd be scalped and skinned before we could get halfway there."

"Oh, hell," Jack said. "Come on through, but leave the hole small as possible. We got to plug it with something."

So the pick-axe worked again, and the hole started growing, and after about fifteen minutes it was wide enough for two men to come through, and then Olds pushed his wife through the hole like he was shoving a log into a furnace. "She's still out."

"You hit her hard enough," Bat said.

"Naw, she's mostly drunk, but it was a good punch, don't you think?"

"Try that with me," Jack said, "and see how it turns out."

Between his previous comments and then, Jack had turned chivalrous.

Mr. Olds slipped through. "Naw, I only like to fight people I know I can whip, if I take them by surprise. Me and her have tussled before, and I mostly win. Hell, she cut me pretty bad, you want to know."

"No one's asking," Billy Dixon said.

When they was all through that hole, me and a few of the others went in there and grabbed some supplies, a barrel of water, some jerky and some bags of beans, and when we got that inside the saloon, we put sacks of grain that was in the saloon at the hole and pushed an anvil that was in the corner, being there for no reason I could figure, up against them. It wasn't much, but it was something. They came through that hole, they'd have to come one at a time, unless they took time to break down the wall. If they started on that, we'd pull aside them sacks and start on them.

"I Got A Hand In My Ass here was just telling us about some Indian magic, wasn't you?" Jack said turning back to Happy Collins.

"It's I Got A Hand In My Hair, but Happy will do," he said.

"Go on with your story, Ass," Jack said.

Happy sighed. "Quanah has them all wound up tight as a cheap watch. He's told them how this medicine man, this White Eagle—"

"That's your father-in-law?" one of the men asked.

"No. My father-in-law is White Shield. White Eagle is a medicine man."

"Just tell it," Jack said.

"White Eagle said he has enough magic to take care of the whole of the Indian nations, except the Tonkawa. Nobody has much for them. Comanche, pretty much everyone else, thinks they're toadies for the whites and are said to be cannibals. White Eagle told the others that he had a vision. That he went up in the heavens and seen the Great Spirit, and the Great Spirit told him he was going to lead the Indians against the whites and drive them out. He even got the Comanche doing the Sundance, way the Cheyenne do. You know the Comanche, they are the orneriest bunch of warriors this side of Genghis Khan, but they went for it like a perch on a cricket. That Sundance, that is painful business. I have watched it a few times, but have never had any urge to do it. It is best seen from afar."

I ought to pause here and lay this out to some of you so you'll know what he was talking about.

What the Cheyenne called the Sundance was that they had bones or sticks stuck through their breasts, and then rawhide strands was tied to them, and then long strands to a pole that was stuck up in the ground. Some of them would take a buffalo skull and tie it to bones ran through the meat in their backs. The skulls made them heavy, made them fall back and pull against the bones through their breasts, those rawhide strands. They danced and chanted and pulled back until the bones or sticks snapped out of their chests, or some of the other Indians would tug on them, helping break them loose. During this time they was supposed to have a vision. I know I'd have one or two, and most of it would be trying to figure out how I had got talked into such a thing in the first place.

"I'll say," Bat said.

"He told them if they attack with full vigor, they will win and will not be bothered by your bullets."

"So far he's not a shining light," Jack said.

"I agree," Happy said. "I think that's why they've backed off for the moment, trying to figure what to do, what went wrong."

Billy, who was at a window looking out, talking over his shoulder, said, "Which is which here, Hand In The Ass?"

Happy didn't even bother to correct, just sighed, got up at a stoop and made his way to the window.

"Who is who?" Billy asked.

I had eased over too, my curiosity being stronger than my common sense. It was quite a view, all them

Comanche bunched up on a hill near a mile away. Happy studied the crowd up there, said, "One ain't got no drawers on of any kind, just swinging it in the wind, painted yellow, that's White Eagle."

"He doesn't seem to have much faith in his own medicine," I said. "He's got some distance there."

"They have all sort of made for the rear," Billy said, "and I know that ain't from lack of courage."

"No," Jack said, as he came over for a peek. "It is not, but they don't like surprises. They see signs in deer shit and flying birds and most anything. If they think the sign is good and it ain't, it pees in their soup. They have to take time to wrap their head around it. Right now, they're up there figuring how they're going to kill us. If they was mad before, they are more mad now."

"That's right," Happy said. "That's how they are. But if they decide things was not just right, or White Eagle can tell them something that soothes the fact that they lost a few warriors, in spite of his assurances, they will come on, and it will be busy."

"Who is that next to White Eagle?" I said that as a big Indian on a white horse had ridden up, and was looking out on us.

"That there is Quanah his ownself," Happy said. "There aren't any chiefs that run all things for the Comanche, or the Cheyenne neither, but him and White Eagle is close to it as of these days. They don't like the

way things are going and are trying to group up and
have leaders. I note my father-in-law has hung to the
back, even farther back than White Eagle. That was
something that was said of him, from time to time. That
he liked a good fight when he and his warriors outnum-
bered their enemies, but that he had a tendency to linger
otherwise. He's lingering. I don't see any of the other
leaders... Oh, wait a minute, there's Robert. He is kind
of hunkered down over his horse. He does that when he's
pissed about things. I figure he's mad at White Eagle,
and I figure White Eagle is pretty much aware he's in the
shit house now."

QUANAH PARKER WAS part Comanche and part white. The son of Cynthia Ann Parker, who was stolen when she was a child, and became a squaw of a Comanche named Nocona, which made him a Scotch-Irish Comanche, though they wasn't as rare as you might think. The Comanche was among the most common for killing everybody and their dog, cattle, and keeping only horses and children if they wasn't babies, and therefore trouble. Them they would kill as quick as too many cats, banging their brains out or sticking them on cactus and such. They wasn't a sentimental sort. But the children that was older they'd sometimes keep as slaves, or add into the tribe, as their numbers was declining due to disease from frontier folks and rifle shot, as well as folks like us killing their traveling grocery stores.

Cynthia was rescued some many years later, having bore Quanah, and another son, if memory serves me, and a little daughter named Prairie Flower. She wasn't all that happy about being rescued, though. She had been taken so young, she didn't know shit about the whites, outside of remembering she was Cynthia Ann Parker. That didn't stop white folks from making her stay with them, though. They was certain wasn't nothing better in the world than being a white person, living the way they wanted you to live. I understood a bit of her concern, having been among whites as a young slave. On the frontier, I was better treated, and by some folks a lot better. Buffalo hunters and mountain men was down right democratic compared to others, even Yankees. Therefore I can see her being more than a smidgen nervous amongst the whites.

She run off a few times, but they wouldn't let her go, caught her and brought her back. Her baby died, and then she died too. Starved herself to death. After she was taken, Quanah never saw her again. She died four years before this time I'm telling you about, and I apologize. I can't seem to stick to anything straight away, and get distracted as easily as a cow by a blue bottle fly.

So there we was, surrounded by hundreds of Indians, and we was now less than thirty, some having died in the wagons outside. A couple of the men that had been wounded wasn't doing so well either, and there was a couple that was talking about putting on the sneak if we could hold until dark. There was also a man or two thinking about breaking out in broad daylight for the horses and making a run for it. This was something that got our best wishes, but not our support, especially that whole daylight runaway plan. Besides, the horses had at this point either been taken by the Indians, scattered, or shot in the barrage of gunfire that had gone on earlier. They wouldn't be waiting politely for us in the corral.

It wasn't that I didn't consider escape plans, but outside of tunneling straight down to China, nothing seemed better than those rickety walls, the hunters and those buffalo rifles, me and my pistols and that sweet Winchester.

Well, there I was contemplating, thinking that the bullet I ought to save for myself ought to be that 4/10 load. I figured I put the barrel in my mouth and let it rip, there wouldn't be any wounding and surviving, left to be worked over by the Comanche, Cheyenne, and Kiowa. I would be missing a head. One thing I decided I would do, if time allowed, was shave my head. A good load from the 4/10 might make my part a bit too wide for scalping, but I didn't want to leave my hair to hang on their scalps. I was a Negro with what we called good hair. I wore it long because it made me look like a real frontiersman, which I was, and the girls liked it. Also, it covered my ears, which was a little like two ends of a hallway with the doors thrown open.

I pulled my knife and was going to get some water from one of the water barrels, and then I realized we needed all the water there was to drink, not wasted on me shaving my head. I put the knife away. I hadn't no sooner done that then a barrel was dragged around with a dipper in it, and we all took turns. The man dragging it was the barkeep, and he said, "This here is it, boys. Unless one of you would like to go out to the well."

That got a short laugh.

"They done cut up a horse or some such and dropped down it," Jack said, "you can bet on that. Maybe they all peed in it. That's how they work. How much whisky is there?"

"Plenty," the barkeep said.

"That's what we need," Billy said, "a bunch of us drunk and trying to make a clear shot."

"I been thirsty enough I would have drank piss and thought it a treat," Jack said.

"I'm shooting myself first," Bat said.

"You say that now," Jack said.

"Ask me about it later," Bat said. "See if the view changes."

I eased up by Jack, said, "So, you think this is where we toss in our hats?"

"Could be. Never say never until never is done. Or almost done. You save a load for yourself, Nat."

"Planned on it."

"You know, that fellow ate all the peaches, it was me told him to go to the shitter."

"Everyone has to shit," I said.

"That's true, but I told him right then. Maybe it was his pancreas."

"He'd have gone to the outhouse soon enough," I said. "It's just how it all shook out."

"Reckon so," Jack said.

Then Olds got our attention. He called out, "They come, bet you they come through the roof. That's the weak part."

No one disagreed with that.

Olds put his hands on his hips and looked up at the ceiling. "There's still a hole where that support pole cracked. I think I can ladder up there for a peek, see when they're coming. My head will be between the support poles, and the sod is pushed up there, so I might get a look-see before they note me up there."

"All right," Bat said. "But you ought to let me do it. I'm a bit more nimble than you."

"You ain't nothing but a green kid," Olds said.

I looked around for Mrs. Olds, see how she felt about such concerning her husband, but she was still on the floor asleep. The Indians could be scalping her and cutting off her toes, and she wouldn't have known no difference. She was drunk as anyone I'd ever seen and snoring like wind blowing through the mountains.

Olds got a Henry rifle from the stock against the wall, and Billy pulled a ladder from behind the bar, and propped it up.

"I'll just go up there for a gander," Olds said.

"I ought to do it," Bat said. "I'm small. That ladder looks rotten to me."

"I've climbed that ladder many a time and it's held," Olds said.

"That may be why you ought not to climb it anymore," Bat said. "Your fat ass is bound to be wearing it down."

"Oh, go diddle yourself," Olds said.

The ladder was propped and a man held either side of it, me being one of them, and up went Olds, that ladder squeaking like it was in pain. But up he went, hoping to see better what was behind us, as there was no window on that side.

He reached the top, gently poked his head through the hole in the sod, between the two support poles. After a moment he said, "My, my. I can tell you one thing."

"What's that," a man called up.

"There are a lot of fucking Indians out there."

"Thanks for that bit of news," Jack called out from the window.

"I can also say, for whatever reason, they ain't behind us. I figure they got some braves tucked out there in the grass somewhere, but I don't see them. Why ain't they surrounding us?"

"Why should they?" Jack said. "When they charge down off that rise and out from the trees, they'll flow over us like water. We can run for it, but without horses, we wouldn't have a chance. They're doing fine. They can wait us out if they like."

"They won't do that," Happy said. "They are in for the kill, and are hot for it. I think they are holding back a little due to some disappointment. They was all supposed to be untouchable. Meaning bullets wouldn't hit them. They are now uncertain, and the medicine man will have to make excuses for the ones that got killed. I saw him this morning looking for a sign, which meant he knew he had got himself on the edge of a cliff with them predictions. I was figuring that right then, before I was asked to run like hell. He gave the braves instructions on how they were to conduct themselves, and if he can prove someone killed a skunk, which is bad medicine when on the war path, then he can claim they are the ones threw off the magic. Medicine man has not only got to come up with predictions, he's got to plan excuses for when things go wrong. It's part of the job."

Olds called down. "Still a lot of Indians... Wait now. Here's something. Two riders coming this way, way off, and they ain't Indians."

"Well," said Jimmy, "they're skint."

Right then the ladder squealed and a rung cracked, and down come Olds, and he hit the ground in such a way his gun went up under his chin, and obviously being set on a hair trigger, the jar set it off, sending a round through chin and out the top of his head. He didn't move a inch after that. Wasn't no kicking or moaning, he was dead as a bag of hammers.

Jack turned from the window at the sound of the shot, seen Olds on the ground, men gathering around him. Jimmy said, "Well, he's out of it."

Bat scurried up the ladder without weapons, avoiding the missing rung, and when he was up there, Billy said, "Here go, Bat," and handed him the Henry Olds had dropped.

I glanced over to Mrs. Olds, but she wasn't aware her husband was dead. She wasn't aware of anything. For all she cared she was dead.

If it seems we sort of took this all in stride, we didn't. It wasn't that we wasn't caring, but we had learned to put that sort of thing in our vest pocket, or most of us had. We could save our upset feelings for when we could afford them.

Bat yelled down, "Those two are coming Hell-Bent-For Leather, but I don't think they're going to beat the Indians. There's a wad of them coming around to the side of them, on their left."

We heard a couple of shots then.

"There's ten, maybe twelve Indians on them. Oh, shit. One of their horses stumbled... Ah, hell, the other tumbled over it. I think one took a shot, and the other is up, got a broke leg way it's standing. Those two's scalps are good as taken."

"I'm going out after them," I said. "Open them doors."

"Son," Jack said. "You can't."

"I can and I am."

"Niggers can run," Jimmy said. "Only one of us got a chance of doing it. I only knew two niggers couldn't run. One of them had a bad leg and the other had a wrenched back. No offense, Nat."

"A little taken," I said.

"They're to the right of the doors, and way out there, not so far you wouldn't be able to make it easy enough if you were on a picnic and there were no Indians," Bat said. "I'd stick, Nat."

"Open the doors and keep your eyes and ears on," I said.

They pulled the planking and the doors came open. With rifle in hand, away I did run.

{7}

I AM A FAST runner, but I made a note that if me and Jimmy didn't get killed, I was going to punch him in the mouth.

Went for all I was worth, I can assure you of that, and it was fairly flat there, so I had a mighty smooth run, considering the circumstances. I knew that Bat wouldn't fire at those Indians near that pair until necessary, because when he did, they might note I was coming. Right then they was concentrated on sending arrows and shots at them two out there on the ground. Soon as they noticed me, he would commence if he was thinking clear, and maybe not even then. I might be out of reasonable range. But when I started back, and with them coming after me, because I assumed they would, he could cut down on them then. I had no doubt he would.

I could see the limping horse and the one already down, and I seen one of the men stand from behind the dead horse, grab the injured horse's bridle, put a pistol to its head and bring it down in such a way that a V was created with the two dead animals. That was smart thinking.

The Indians, and they looked like a small band of Kiowas, was riding up fast now, and when they seen me, an easier target than someone behind a horse, they started firing. I fired back on the run, cock-firing that Winchester until it was empty, hitting two Indians, maybe killing one, and dropping four horses, throwing their riders in the grass. About that same time Bat started shooting that Henry.

The Kiowas dropped off their horses and left them, got behind their dead ones and started shooting arrows and gunfire. By that time I was near the V that fellow had made with the dead mounts, the person who had killed the horse turned to look at me. I had already been noticed, of course, all that gunfire had drawn attention to me.

"I'm coming in," I said.

I took a leap, landed between the two horses. A series of arrows plunked into the dead animals and their hides sputtered with bullets. When I was down between the horses, I seen the survivor was a woman. She had her hair pushed up under her hat, but there was no denying she was a woman, young, in her twenties like me. A white woman with a bit of dark hair showing under her hat.

I turned to look at her partner. He was stretched out on his back with his hands at his sides, like maybe he had laid down for a short nap.

"My brother," she said. "They've killed him."

I had already taken to pulling shells out of my gun belt, slipping them into my Winchester. I said, "Listen here, I'm sorry, but we can't hang our thoughts on that right now. We're going to have to run like rabbits in a second. We stay here, all them other Indians are going to be on us. They can't get them that's in the saloon, they'll settle for us for now. So we're going to run, and as we come up out of here, we got to be shooting their way, even if we can't take time to aim. We got to make them nervous and busy ducking, and we got to move, run for all we're worth."

"All right," she said.

"What's your name?" I said.

"Millie."

"Millie, when I say go, do not hesitate, just go."

"I have shot buffalo and been in some scrapes, so you don't wait on me. I got a fully loaded Winchester, and I will not go down easy."

"Good then," I said.

I took a deep breath, said, "Go."

Away we went. It was one hell of a run. I kept thinking in the back of my mind I was going to step in a hole and go down, or catch a bullet or some arrows in the back, but when we come up out of there we come up firing. As we ran, I turned and started running backwards, and firing my Winchester, and I was good at it. I used to do it on the farm for fun, run backwards like that, and I could even out-run some of the other kids running like that, so maybe Jimmy was onto something about colored being able to run, but still, I was going to punch him in the mouth. I fired at those redskins like I truly hated them, which I didn't. There wasn't any use in that. They was who they was, same as me. I had been whipped as a child slave for nothing more than spilling milk. I had been told if I got a cold and gave it to a white person it was worse than if a white person gave it to you. That I was second to everything in life, and that's why I had come west. I let all that anger cover me like a shield. It wasn't a real shield and it wouldn't have stopped a gnat from flying through, but it was everything that had ever made my blood boil, and before I realized it I had emptied that Winchester and was cocking on empty.

I wheeled then, found that Millie was really hauling freight, was more than halfway to the doors. I run to catch up with her, shifted the empty Winchester to my left hand, drew the LeMatt, and come even with her.

Millie's hat blew off and her black hair popped out in a long trail, like ink blown in the wind, and now there came a sound from the warriors up on the hill and behind us. They wanted Millie because they knew there wasn't no greater humiliation to a man than to rape his women to death. It was better than cutting off their balls, far as they was concerned. So they come then in a sea of Indians, Quanah leading, riding down from the rise ahead of us, others whooping it up behind us, some rushing on foot. Out from the creek come more Indian stragglers.

The swarm came, arrows flew, the bullets tore holes in the air. It looked like we was as good as nabbed, and I was preparing to shoot Millie, then myself, when the doors to the store opened. There came from that open doorway, and from the roof where Bat was, a withering round of Sharps rifle fire. There was screams and yells, thunks and thuds, and flurries of sod being thrown up as men and critters struck and rolled on the ground.

I was in fear of being shot down by our own bunch.

To the left of me, having circled the walls, came a handful of riders, and one of them fired a shot that tore through the top of my left shoulder, burned like a branding iron. I cross-fired with my right hand, shot his horse through the neck, and down that horse went, almost sliding into me. I can't tell you much after that, but I emptied that 9 shooter, and clicked the baffle for

the 4/10 load. We were almost through the doors of the store now. Men filled it from side to side. Me and Millie was running low. Our people was firing over our heads, just to keep a stream of lead in the air, then they parted and Millie made it through.

A crazy Indian come off from my right and was about to grab me. I fired that 4/10 load in his face. Then I was inside and the doors was being slammed, the wooden bar thrown back into place. Outside came a ferocious pounding of arrows and gun shots and fists. Bullets tore through the door and made holes that light peeked through and the room was riddled with these sticks of light.

Inside, Millie had gone to the window, was standing by Jack, firing her pistol. I knelt down on the ground and reloaded my weapons, went to another window where a man had just fallen, stuck the Winchester out and started firing, not so fast this time, and more accurately. Bullets was plunking into the walls, tearing through in places, pieces of adobe flying around, and then—

It was over.

FOR THE TIME being anyway.

Them Indians had regrouped out there on that ridge, feeling good about being just out of rifle shot. One naked brave stood up on horseback, turned his back toward us, and showed us his ass. No one took a shot at him. Too far.

Then Quanah rode up, and so did White Eagle, all naked and yellow-coated with clay. They sat on their horses side by side, checking out the battlefield. What they saw was a pile of dead Indians. We had lost a few ourselves, along with Olds and that fellow out there lying dead between the V of those horses, but them Indians had taken a beating.

Bat called down from his perch, "They are chopping up that dead man at the horses."

He meant Millie's brother.

"Oh, the goddamn savages," she said.

All the men had now noted that she was not only a woman, but that she was one who spoke right up and didn't faint.

Jack said, "She shot two of them Indians with good pistol shots. I think she might have killed one of them, and the other will be lying mighty still later tonight, as he took one in the balls I think."

It was a compliment that you gave a man, not a woman. Least not normally.

"She did all right out there too," I said. "I think she dropped a couple."

Millie heaved a little, like she was going to cry, but then she cinched it up.

"She can run too," Bat called down, "sort of lopes like an antelope," and then he come down the ladder. His hat was full of bullet holes and his face had been streaked with cuts from where shots had come close. He didn't seem in the least fazed about having been nearly shot-up, but when he was on the ground he took a good look at Millie, and that fazed him. She was a pretty thing, and about as on the far end of womanhood from Mrs. Olds, who was still peacefully sleeping, than a buffalo is from a deer. She wore buckskins that fit her loose, but you could tell there was something nice and soft under them, and her hair was long and tumbled down her back and there was something about the way it swung that roused the blood. She looked taller than she was, as she was wearing boots, and those boots cocked her ass up nicely. It doesn't sound very gentlemanly to talk in this manner, but none of us was gentlemanly right then. We all figured our days were numbered, so we enjoyed our last moments by really giving her the once over.

Then she knocked the wind out of us.

"Listen, you piss-ants," she said, "I have ridden the trail and fought Indians before, and hunted buffalo, and I can ride like an Indian, shoot like Wild Bill Hickok, and drink like a fish, but I do not sell myself, and I'm not for free unless I choose it, so any of you fellows get the wrong idea, you'll be wearing your nose on the other side of your face, if you don't end up with a bullet in the head. Are we understood?"

We all agreed that things were well understood.

Jack, still at the window said, "Look at this."

Those of us who could get to the windows in time and was willing to take a chance on there not being some Indians hid close, flocked over there, shoving and pushing for a look. There was a fistful of Indians dragging White Eagle off his horse. They had sticks, and when he was on the ground they went about beating the pure-dee dog shit out of him.

Binoculars was found, a couple pairs, and a bunch of us got a look, but even from that distance there was a clear view without them. You could easily make out what was going on, and what you couldn't make out, you could figure on.

One of those who had managed a window view was Happy, a.k.a. I Have A Hand In My Hair, and he said, "They've decided White Eagle's magic failing the way it did wasn't just because someone killed a skunk or shit on a scared rock, or some such. They have decided it failed because White Eagle is full of that which comes loose from a goose, and they are teaching him a lesson."

"It's a good one too," Jack said.

It was indeed a good lesson. Sticks was coming down on his ass so hard and fast, it looked like Chinamen hammering down spikes on the railroad. This went on until they was tired, and then they rested on their sticks. White Eagle wallowed around on the ground for awhile. Then he got to his feet, went to his horse, and tried to pull himself up on it, but that was when Quanah turned with the rifle he was holding, and shot the horse in the head, causing it to topple and nearly fall over on White Eagle, who proved spry enough after that beating to dodge the falling critter, which fell with its legs kicking and shit spewing out of its ass. I really don't know about the last part. It was a good distance, but that's usually how it was.

The Indians with the sticks was rested now, and so they came again, and damn if I didn't start to feel sorry for White Eagle. It was a serious thumping.

While all this was going on, another Indian come riding up to sit on his horse by Quanah, and then another, and while they was beginning to clutch up on the hill, some more Indians took to chopping up White Eagle's horse, and now they was all pulling out their johnsons and pissing on White Eagle while he lay on the ground.

"They sure don't like him," Millie said.

"Seems that way," Jack said.

Billy was watching all of this quietly. He said, "I got a fifty, but I want to borrow one of those 50-90's, someone's got one to loan me. I'm going to take a shot."

"Too far away," Jimmy said.

"Yeah, but I'm of a mind to do it anyway," Billy said.

Bets went around about how many yards or feet the bullet would fall short, some money, pocket knives and a cigar went into a hat.

Billy took the fifty in one hand, wet his finger, poked it out the window for a second, pulled it back, "Said wind's not kicking, so what the hell."

He laid the rifle on the window frame, coughed once, wiggled his ass and shifted his feet, said, "Now, don't nobody say nothing."

"You couldn't hit anything up there if we was a hundred feet closer," said Jimmy. "Give me that hat. I got more money to put in against this shot."

"He said shut up," Millie said. "He don't make the shot, I'll pull the wagon with any and everyone of you, long as I'm allowed rest time."

Everyone shut up and was hopeful of Billy having the bad eye, all except me. I had bet on his side of the matter, but only in my head. Billy did the thing with his feet again, got his ground, leaned into the Sharps, and with both eyes open, took his aim.

He pulled the trigger. The Indian to the right of Quanah fell off his horse, and then the sound of the shot echoed against the ridge. Well now, there was a bit of excitement up there. Them Indians thought for sure they was out of range, them being about a mile away, and frankly, so did all of us, and that included Billy.

"Well fuck a hairy goat ass," Billy said.

"That's a relief," Millie said, "I was already trying to figure if there was axel grease in the house. You missed that shot, at some stage here in the day or night, figured I might need it."

"Holy shit," Jack said. "That is the most amazing goddamn shot I've ever seen. Except for one I made once where I shot the Sunday hat off God's head."

Everyone laughed. It was like we had all bottled up something and could uncork it now.

Up there on the hill the Indians was gathering their dead man, and riding away, all except Quanah who sat on his horse and looked down at us. I know he was too far away to tell for sure, but you can bet his eyes was blazing.

Course, White Eagle was still on the ground. And while Quanah sat there, we saw White Eagle rise and wobble away, heading in the direction the others had gone. I figured he had a few more beatings to catch up with.

After a moment Quanah lifted his rifle and fired a shot in the air, let out with a whoop, wheeled his horse and was gone.

"You should have took a shot at him," Jimmy said, now an enthusiastic supporter of Billy and that rifle.

"Naw, it was a scratch shot, and a good one, and if I missed next time, it would be said I was lucky. Which I was. I think what helped me there was they was all bunched up together, and maybe a wind kicked up at the back of my shot, pushing. But still, it was a good shot, wasn't it?"

"It was," Jack said, and clapped Billy on the shoulder.

We all stood there for awhile, and then Happy said, "They have had enough."

"Maybe," Jimmy said.

"No," Happy said. "They are through. The magic failing, that long shot, and that was Black Buffalo Hump you killed. He's one of the more respected Comanche. You took the wind out of their sails. With their magic coming apart like that, they think that shot is a sign

[85]

from the Great Spirit that White Eagle was a false prophet as well as an asshole."

"A sore false prophet," Jack said. "I bet them sticks left marks."

"Hey, Jimmy," I said.

"What?"

When he turned toward me I hit him as hard as I could, knocking him down into wherever Mrs. Olds was keeping her soul.

THAT WAS IT for what has come to be called the Second Battle of Adobe Walls, but it wasn't over for me and Black Hat Jack, or for that matter Millie.

After the battle, what bodies the Indians didn't collect, some of the men hacked up or pissed on or did pretty much the same thing to the bodies the Comanche and their partners had done to the whites. Neither me nor Jack took part in that, though Millie did so to avenge her brother, though when she was finished doing what she did with a hatchet, her brother was still dead, and the Indian she had chopped on hadn't been taught any sort of lesson that I could understand. Anyway, they did that, and the bodies of our men killed was buried, including them in the wagon, along with Millie's brother. They took the Indians out away from Adobe Walls for the crows and vultures and ants to have them.

Mrs. Olds they loaded up in the back of a buffalo wagon with the body of her husband. She didn't never make a move, still being under the influence. She may still be passed out at this very moment, even though some years have passed; that woman was drunk.

During all these goings on, I looked up and saw out on the same ridge where the Indians had been, my horse Satan. He had turned back up and was looking down on us with the same contempt that Quanah had. He could be like that. I told you how he would come to my whistle when he was in the mood. Well, thing was he wasn't in the mood right then, cause I wore myself out trying to whistle him up. He just stood there looking, like he had no idea what I was doing, or who I was.

I found my saddle and started out after him, and Jack decided he'd come along and help. He'd found his horse easy enough, saddled it. He loaded up my spare saddle bags full of ammunition, flapped them across his horse, over his own bullet-filled bags, and rode along with me as I walked, that heavy saddle on my back.

I guess because I was the one who rescued her, Millie decided she'd go along with us, ending up on the back of Jack's horse.

Carrying a saddle like that is hot and heavy work, and about the time I got to the creek, I put the saddle under a tree. And then, just carrying the bridle, decided I'd go on after Satan and ride him back to the saddle bareback.

I gave my Winchester to Jack to strap on his horse, and I just wore my handguns. The Indians did appear to be gone, but you couldn't be sure, and my damn horse seemed to be heading out toward the way they went. I decided if he went too far, I was just going to have to let him go and see if he might send me a letter as to his location later in the year.

After a bit, we seen Satan, and he was moving away from us, prancing like he was a wild pony, and in some ways he was.

Finally I decided I'd have to go after him Indian style, which meant I would take hold of Jack's stirrup, and he would get his horse up to a mild run, and I would run along beside the horse, letting its body carry me forward, just being alert enough to get my feet up and make with leaping motions. You could run quite a ways like this if you had the stamina, and I did.

We come to another rise, higher than the one we had gone over. We stopped there to let me get my wind. From that vantage point we could see far in the distance the Indians riding away slowly, going home without some of their dead, their tails between their legs, having been whipped by believing in White Eagle's horseshit. I didn't have a mind to be sad about their circumstances, just then. I still had my hair and was grateful of it. It was that Adobe Walls battle, their loss there, that some said was when the Comanche decided they was finished.

That the buffalo wasn't coming back, no matter if they did the Cheyenne Sundance, believed in medicine men, or force of numbers. Their way of life was pretty much over, as far as Texas went. On up north there was still to come the Battle of Little Big Horn, and that would do in the Sioux and the rest of the Cheyenne, but that was still two years off. What we now call the Wild West was winding down like a worn-out clock.

Those Indians decided us on turning back, letting Satan go his own way. It was while we was going back down that ridge, me clinging to Jack's stirrup, jumping along like a jack rabbit beside his horse, that we come by some buffalo wallows. We paused at the wallow to let me blow and get my breath back. It was at the same time about twenty Indians, mostly Kiowa, come out of what seemed like a straight run of prairie, but was instead a low spot that the grass covered unless you was right on it. They just come riding up as if out of coming up from the center of the earth. We was all surprised. They looked at us, and we looked at them. You could almost see them thinking: Why here are some of those that run us off, and we are twenty and they are three, and one of them is a woman. We are in good shape here.

Thing that worked against them, though, wasn't but two of them was armed with rifles, the rest had bows and arrows. I should point out that those are weapons serious enough. A good bow shooter can set a dozen arrows in flight faster than a man can cock a regular set-up Winchester. I, of course, had a different sort of Winchester, and could fire rounds as fast as I could jack, which gave me a slight edge.

I think them Kiowa decided that the day was going to end on a happier note than they had anticipated. They took to yelling, and as we knew what was coming next, Jack rode his horse down into the buffalo wallow, dismounted, jerked Millie off its back, shot his horse in the head faster than them Indians could figure to ride down on us.

It was the right thing to do. Wasn't no use trying to outrun them Kiowa, not with Millie clinging to the back, and me running alongside. They'd have been on us quick and things would have been over for the three of us before we could have gone a hundred yards.

The horse tumbled back and kicked once, but Jack had pulled it in such a way that its legs was pointing into the wallow, and the depression of its body there gave us something to hide behind, as long as they came from one side. Another thing we had going was the wallow was deep, and there was a deeper depression on the far side, and therefore the rim of the wallow served as a kind of fortification. It wasn't the best you could ask for, but it was more than you could hope to get, all things considered. Of course, we was also hoping all our shooting would bring some of the men still at Adobe Walls on the run, but it also occurred to me that shooting might be just the thing not to bring them. We hadn't told anyone of our plans to chase my horse, and there wasn't any reason they might not think it was the Indians firing off shots in anger. I was more concerned that some of the other Indians, having broken off from the others, like these, would hear the firing and come to the aid of their companions, making short work of us.

I won't bore you with all the shooting we done, as you've already been told how it was at Adobe Walls, and this was more of the same, but with less Indians, though our situation was no less dire. We was three and they was twenty, and we was in a hole in the ground with a dead horse for cover. Before nightfall, that horse was littered with arrows and holes from bullets that had missed their mark. We had killed one of them and two of their horses, to put them afoot, but far as we knew, no stray bullets had put anybody down under. They pulled the rest of their mounts back down the hill out of shooting range, as killing their horses and putting them on foot was a good strategy anytime.

Them Kiowa lying out there in the grass would pop up from time to time and take pot shots at us, but they didn't keep their heads up long. They knew we could shoot.

Why they hadn't tried to crawl around behind us, I can't say. Maybe they wasn't fully committed after being defeated the way they was. They might even have seen some sport in it.

It was a bright night and we could see good, and we was keeping our eyes peeled in a serious manner. I have heard that Indians do not like to fight at night, and that's true of some of them, and to be honest, it's not my first pick neither. You're just as liable to shoot one of your own as one of theirs, getting all worked up by the battle. But again, it wasn't a thought we was holding to, as plenty of Indians have put the sneak on folks at night, and did them in before they knew there was something to be worried about.

Way we was arranged was we was all behind the horse. Jack had pulled the saddle bags with the ammo free, and with it I could load both rifle and pistols. Millie had only a pistol, but she looked determined there in the starlight, and I will admit that her bravery gave me a feeling that might have seemed odd for the moment. There are white men who will cringe to hear this, but I had a mighty strong taste for her right then. I'm not saying even had she been of the same mind at that moment, or that it would have been a smart move for us to drop our drawers and take advantage of romance right then. That would have most certainly led to us having as many arrows in us as that dead horse. But she was mighty fetching there in the starlight, her black hair dangling, her lying on her back, looking away from the horse, watching for any of them Kiowa, coming around behind us.

After awhile, Jack said, "Nat," and he said it in such a way, I knew he was trying to draw me near to him. I inched up, and soon as I did, Millie said, "You might as well tell the both of us outright. It's not like I haven't grown accustomed to bad news, and am fully aware we are in a tight spot, so don't hold the horses."

"If only we had one," Jack said. "I think I did the right thing then with this old nag. She could hardly outrun me. But there's one that might serve to do better, provided there was a distraction. On that rise beyond."

Jack pointed. I turned and seen it was Satan. The bastard was about a quarter mile away, just standing there looking, and in that moment I told myself I caught up with him and was able to ride him out, I was going to shoot him and eat him and have a pair of boots made out of him just on general principle.

"We don't want to draw attention that he's there to them Indians," said Jack. "They may already have seen him, but then again, they have a strong eyeball on us, waiting for us to make a mistake. Another bit of news is I didn't fill my canteen at the creek before we went after Satan. I thought it would be less of a journey. I hoped for water in this wallow, but damn if it don't seem to be dry."

"So we got a possible horse," I said, "but no water. I don't see how a horse would do us good, other than shooting him to hide behind."

"Hell, Nat. Satan, that one is a runner and you know it. There ain't nothing on four feet can catch him."

"Probably true enough," I said.

"Now, there's actually a worse bit of news," Jack said.

"What could be worse?" Millie said.

"Well, they want you, little lady, you know that much," he said.

"I do," Millie said. "There is nothing better to satisfy their taste than the rape and tortured murder of a white woman."

"It is similar to what we have done to their own, so they are even more spiteful about it," Jack said. "And Nat here will tell you about how white folks have treated black slave women, but this ain't the spot for politics, since I ain't running for any kind of office. But considering I may not get to speak on it at another date, I thought I'd toss a loop on it. The other problem I'd like to mention, and this is a personal problem. I caught a bullet a short time back. One of those times they threw a few rounds in this direction. It come over the top of this dead cayuse and caught me in the gut."

"Damn, Jack," I said.

"Bad?" Millie asked.

"I'd say so, yes," Jack said, "which is why I call it bad news. And I didn't even know it right at first. I mean, the pain set in pretty quick, but not right at first. I didn't know for sure what it was. Felt like I'd been stung. I been shot before, but not like this; them was all nothing more than a case of sun burn. Now that the sting has passed, the wolf is here, chewing at my guts. I thought I'd save the information until it became important. As I can feel me draining out, I thought it was time to mention it."

I put my hand on the ground next to Jack. It was dark and the ground was damp and sticky.

"Kept my jacket closed up, even hot as it was, holding in things. Now I'm feeling a might more comfortable, there being a snap in the air, and me being pretty near out of blood."

"We got to get you out of here right away," I said. "I'm not sure how yet, but we got to. You and Millie, you got to take Satan and ride out and let me give them the business for awhile."

"No, Nat, that is right manful of you, but I couldn't ride nowhere. This coat is keeping my guts inside. Not all of what we been smelling is dead horse. My innards are raising quite an aroma."

"Tell me what you want," I said, "and I will try and move heaven and earth, and piss hell's fires out for you."

"I know that, Nat. And I'm going to tell you what you both got to do, and I can't really measure much of an argument from you. You got to listen to me."

"We're listening," Millie said.

Jack looked out over the horse and checked on the Indians. We couldn't see them. For all we knew they were finally sneaking up behind us, or some of them was.

"I don't want to die in a wallow behind a dead horse, leaking out the last of me. I want to die fighting, and I'm going to do that. I don't think I can stand till morning. But there's one small chance, and it depends on the disposition of that goddamn horse of yours, Nat. He looks to me like he may have had his fun and would like to be caught up and taken to some grain, so we'll play it that way. It don't work like that, then it's going to be the same for me either way, and I advise the two of you if there's no fight really left, to do what you got to do; that whole last bullet business."

"That's exactly what I'll do," Millie said.

"Good," Jack said. "I got my rifle here, a pistol and a knife. And what I'm going to do is rise up out of here, if I got the strength to do it, and I'm going to them. Going right at them like a derailed train. I am going to fire the shot in my Sharps and toss it, then go in on them with pistol and knife. I won't live long enough to be tortured, but I just might take a few of them down and give you time to catch that contrary horse. You can bet though I'll keep them busy till Old Man Death comes to collect me up in his croker sack."

"That's crazy, Jack," I said.

"Yeah, it is, but what other plan you got?" he said.

"They'll get tired and go on."

"Might, but they are pretty moved to kill somebody after how things worked out. They'd like to take our scalps back to all them others, and say, boys, you done slid out of there when the doings was still good, and we got the scalps to show it. It would put them in good with their fellows if they killed us and maybe brought Millie in for further activities, such as they are. Maybe they'll just want to rape and kill her here."

"Neither is appealing," Millie said.

"You take that Winchester, saddle bags of ammo, and while I'm up and about my business, whistle up that horse. He don't come, you just keep running. It's a long ways, but you just might get away if luck is on your side and they go blind in both eyes and their legs break and their horses won't mind them."

"Hardly sounds hopeful," I said.

"It isn't. Satan is your best chance, and then you still got to get on him and get out of here riding double. It's all we got, Nat. It's what we're going to do. You two get ready to run."

"Jack," I said. "You know I don't want to leave you."

"I do, and if it was just you, I'd still ask you to do this, cause I'll be dead in an hour or two, if I make it that long, and you'll still be in the same spot. But it's not just you. It's her too. Now here I go."

"Take my Winchester," I said.

"No, you'll need that. I'll be in too close a quarters to use it. We rode some good roads and some bad ones together, you dusky demon, but we rode them like men, didn't we?"

"Reckon so," I said.

"All right, then. You may have to help me up and hope you don't take a bullet. I've gathered myself as much as I can. Soon as I'm over the lip and making noise, you two go for Satan. Go fast as you can. My heart is with you. Help me up now, Nat. I'm going to surprise the shit out of them, but first I got to cinch up this jacket with my belt so my guts don't fall out. That shot has made one hell of a hole."

"I AM GOING TO let the pain have me," Jack said. "I been holding in a yell something terrible, and I am about to let it out, so when you hear it, don't piss yourselves. I am going now."

I grabbed his arm and helped him up. My hand brushed against his hand as he let go of me. It was cold as ice. He stepped up on that horse in a lively manner, as if he was a young'n and full of piss and vinegar. He was one game rooster. Out of the wallow he went, and then he was running, that jacket belted up tight around him at the bottom. He let out with a blood-curdling scream, fired into that grass with the Sharps, threw it aside, and drew his pistol.

Me and Millie was already moving then. I wasn't looking at Jack anymore. We came out of the wallow on the side, me with them saddle bags full of ammunition thrown over my shoulder, the dead horse's bridle there too, carrying my Winchester. We ran toward Satan, who stood in his spot, tossing his head. He had gone to nickering too, and I hadn't gone but a few steps when I tried to whistle, but my mouth was too dry. I didn't stop though, just kept running, Millie beside me. Any moment I expected Satan to bolt, and there we'd be, out of what protection the wallow offered and on foot.

Behind us Jack's pistol was popping something furious. I heard gunfire from the Kiowa too. I glanced back once, and them Kiowa was all over Jack, like coyotes trying to take down an old buffalo bull. They was swinging hatchets and clubs and knifes, but Jack, bad off as he was, was making a hell of a stand of it. He had lost that black buffalo hat, no longer had his pistol, but was gripping his skinning knife instead. It flashed in the starlight as it went up and down and slashed right and left.

When I turned back to what was at hand, here come Satan, trotting toward us like he had just been waiting on us. He come right up to me and nickered. I gave Millie my Winchester to hold, patted his nose, then put that bridle on him. I swung up on his back, stuck out my hand, and pulled Millie up behind me.

We was facing the Kiowa then, and I felt mounted I could do Jack some good, come swooping down on them, but it was too late. I saw him fall beneath a rain of blows. But I'll say this for Jack, their numbers was

thinner now. Jack had killed three of them that I could see. The live ones was shoving at one another now, competing for who was going to take Jack's scalp.

Turning Satan with a touch of the reins, I put my heels to him and he began to fly.

Millie said, "They're coming."

I turned to look. Four of those Kiowa was coming after us, having lost interest in Jack now, and maybe lost the tussle over his scalp. They was excited and whooping and really urging their horses.

I hooked my right heel into Satan, swung out to my left so that I was hanging way out from him, him at a full gallop. I had the reins in my teeth. I hung out there in the wind and cocked my Winchester. I didn't have the baffle down, so I cocked and took my time. I aimed and squeezed off easy, and though the world was jumping, my timing was right on. I shot one of them off his horse, and then the others began to slow, and then they was dots way back behind us. I swung back in position, and away we did ride.

Pegasus his ownself couldn't have caught us.

{ 11 }

WE STOPPED AT the creek by Adobe Walls, got my saddle, couple of canteens from the store, filled them from the creek. We got jerky out of there too, blankets, some odds and ends, and continued on, still double on Satan.

As we rode along I wasn't thinking about getting scalped as much as before, and I became aware of Millie's arms around my waist. She leaned her body and head into my back. I could feel her warmth and her breath on the back of my neck. Even with all we had been through, and her in those dirty clothes, she smelled sweeter than a spring flower.

That night we camped and she cried and I just lay on my bed roll across the way and let her do so without saying anything. Finally she got cried out and said, "I wanted to be a tom boy until yesterday. I was good at it.

I ran off to go hunting with my brother. I shot buffalo and skinned them, and I went dirty and nasty for weeks at a time. I fought off men who wanted to get in my britches, or fought off those thought I ought not wear men's clothing. I did all that and I was fine with it until Zeke got killed. That took the starch out of my drawers, right there, that's what I've got to tell you."

"That's understandable," I said.

"Do you think I did wrong as a woman to go out west with my brother and do things like I've done?"

"I hadn't given it any thought," I said. "I think it's fine whatever you do, long as you don't steal something or kill somebody doesn't have it coming, be mean to animals, unless you have to kill and hide behind them or eat them. I think you do okay. You got sand. I can say that for you. You got more guts than a lot of men I known. Back there in that wallow, you was strong, girl, strong. You don't buckle down and hope for the best. You fight your way out."

"You have saved me twice, Nat. Both times I was being attacked by Indians and was with a dead horse. Once two of them."

"Jack saved you the second time, saved me too."

"I didn't mean to sound like I'd forgotten him."

"I know you haven't. How could you? How could anyone?"

"He was brave," she said.

"I'd have died behind that horse," I said. "I'd have just bled out before I'd have done what he done. That took guts."

"I think you'd have done it had it been you shot, Nat. I think you would have."

"That makes one of us."

She got quiet for awhile, said, "Do you think it's wrong for whites and Indians to be together, you know, to marry?"

"I got nothing against it," I said. "Jack had an Indian wife. I never met her, but he held her dear to him. Digging Wolf she was called. They wasn't never married in an American way, but in an Indian way they was. She died of some kind of white man disease. He missed her everyday, talked about her all the time. I reckon he liked her just fine, and she was Indian. Course, I'm not sure if Jack might have been part Indian, or even colored. I don't know."

"Do you think it's okay colored and Indians mix up like that?"

"You mean be together?"

"Yeah."

"I can't see no difference in that than in a white and an Indian or a mixed up blood like Jack. He once told me that somewhere along the line all our blood has mingled."

"How about colored and whites, what you think about that?"

"It don't bother me none, but it sure bothers some, you can count on that."

"What about me and you?" she said.

"I'm going to ask you to explain that one."

"What if I was to take off my pants and come over there and get under your blankets with you?"

"I think I'd have a hard time keeping my own pants on."

"That's what I was hoping for," she said.

She got up then, standing there in the starlight, already barefoot, her boots beside her blankets. She went to unbuttoning her pants. I started to tell her I hadn't meant what I said, and she ought to stop. I knew that was the right thing to say, cause no matter how much the color line didn't bother me, it would damn sure bother whites. But I didn't say anything. I couldn't. My heart was in my mouth.

Well, she slipped off her pants, and her shirt hung down over her womanhood, and then she unbuttoned that and threw it open. I could see her breasts and I could see the darkness between her legs, and then she came to me. I threw back my blanket and she laid down. As I had predicted, my pants came off.

The next few days was a delight, and I remember them as clearly as if they happened this morning. Sometimes I think I can smell her. She had that sweet smell I talked about, and she smelled even better when she was hot and at it. That kind of wild animal smell dipped in mint and lilac water.

We traveled slow, moving everyday farther away from Indian country. That's not to say we dropped our guard, but it is to say we frequently dropped our pants. I worried about getting her with child, and was careful as I could be not to, cause if ever I would have been creating a sad little bastard, it would have been that poor, little fellow. Half white and half black and not too popular with either crowd.

Considering all that happened to us, we was reasonably festive. Or more likely, we was that way on account of what had happened to us. I knew that was what most of Millie's interest was about. We had come close to death, and now we was celebrating life, and doing it with all our abilities.

When we come to a town, there was some men who come up to us right quick, looking angry, wanting to know what a nigger was doing with a white gal snuggled up behind him. Nothing sets a white Texan off his feed quicker than the thought that a colored might be dipping his rope in a white woman's well, which as I said before was one of my great worries. Things could have got testy, but when they started asking, rumbling about what we was doing, Millie slid down off Satan, praised the lord, said how glad she was to see them, said how I had been kind enough to help her, had given her a ride back from the Battle of Adobe Walls and fought Indians for her.

At first they didn't believe her, but she went to telling about her brother, and how things had gone for us, about Billy Dixon's shot. By this time all that news had already been heard, and they took her story to be true, which it was for the most part.

Millie told them too about the fight at the buffalo wallow, and how Jack had died. When she come to that part she tossed in some sniffles, which I like to think was sincere. If not, they was damn well convincing, cause men took off their hats, and women, who had gathered around us, wept. A young boy wanted to know if we got to see Jack scalped. I wanted to scalp that little shit, but held my tongue and held my piece.

She didn't mention what we had been doing under our blankets the last few days. I was just a colored man who had been at the fight and helped her out. I was immediately branded a good nigger, got some pats on the back, and was offered a dinner, as long as I didn't come in the house to eat it. It was a long shot from being out there on the prairie with men who lived by gun and knife. Coming back into civilization I found it had less civilized behavior. Them old boys out there in the wilds could be rude and smelly, forget to wash their hands now and again, but they at least stood back a bit and was willing to take a man's measure. Here, though they took off their hats and didn't spit in public and cleaned under their nails at least once a week, I was already measured, cut and folded. I was a colored man, and though I had done good, I was still a colored. Had I reached out and touched Millie, even on the arm, in a familiar way, I'd have had done to me pretty much what those Comanche had done to that hunter me and Jack found.

Millie got taken to a couple's house to clean up. I had to take my horse to the livery, and then I was blessed to sit on the front porch where the family that had taken her in lived. I sat there watching the sun set with a yellow cat for a companion.

A woman brought me out a supper of cold corn-bread and some warm beans. A moment later she came out with a saucer and a bottle of milk, and poured the cat some of it in the saucer. Now both animals were fed.

From the porch I could look through the windows. The lamps gave the rooms inside a nice glow. Millie sat at the dinner table with the family. She now wore a fine white dress, her black hair washed and combed, mounded up on her head and pinned. Her neck was long and slim, her shoulders narrow and straight. The light lay on her smooth face as if it was a thin coat of gold paint. She was very lovely.

When she moved her hands, shifted in her chair as she talked, she did so in a delicate way, like a woman that had never stepped one foot out of a parlor. Like a woman who had never shot a buffalo or skinned one, had never fought Indians, or nearly died in a wallow out on the prairie.

I could hear them talking. I heard the man and woman asking her about her family, and Millie telling them her brother had been all she had, and now he was dead and she was all alone. She talked about how she had to survive on the trail because that's what her brother wanted. He was the one had her dress like a man so she wouldn't be noticed as a woman right off. He had her do it as a form of protection. She said it was a hard thing, but her brother was all she had, and she had to do his bidding. She didn't mention what she had told me on the trail, about how she had gone off to be different. She damn sure didn't mention what me and her did under them blankets. She spoke kindly of me, the way you might a stray dog.

I knew what she was doing. All that time in pants with a six-gun had worn thin to her. She was trying to find her way back into feminine graces and polite society. Some place where it didn't rain on your head and the wind didn't blow cold and you didn't need to go hunting for your supper and maybe fight a bear or an Indian over it.

I looked at her for a long time, and then she happened to look toward the window. I think she could see me sitting out there in the dark. She looked briefly, then looked away, like she had seen something disturbing, and in a way she had. Now that she was among white people, and I was no longer a warm comfort on a cold, dark night, she felt she had to look at things different. I didn't blame her. There was nothing to come of it, me and her, even if it had meant anything to her, and maybe it had at the time. She had been brave about the color line out there on the plains under the stars with no one to see us but the wildlife, but she couldn't be like that now, not here in a well-lit house, wearing a nice, clean dress. Not where a couple might take her in and make her days more pleasant.

I didn't know exactly how to feel, but in a strange way, I think I wished I was back in that wallow, fighting it out with them Kiowa. I realized I felt more at home there than here.

I finished up eating and left the plate on the porch, gave the cat a pat, and walked over to what served as the livery, which is where I had left Satan. It was one small building and looked to have been put up in a windstorm, way it sagged. It could house three horses and a couple of men if they didn't swing their arms any. There was some covered sheds out to the side, and that's where Satan had ended up. I had wanted to shoot him and eat him before, but now I was glad to have him back.

The livery operator asked that I tell him about the fight out there on the prairie, as he had missed the story first hand. I did the best I could to not be impatient. I told it, and I was sure to build up the white boys more than myself. He let me have my horse for free, including the grain Satan had eaten, and even gave me a bit for the road. He told me that the couple Millie was with had lost their daughter to the influenza. I told him they might well have found another daughter this very night.

I mounted up and rode away, and I never saw Millie again, though along the trail for many days after, I would think of her and our blankets out there on the trail, and those thoughts made me feel good.

﹛ 12 ﹜

SOME YEARS LATER when I was working as a Marshal for Hanging Judge Isaac Parker, I was walking along a boardwalk in Fort Smith, Arkansas, proudly wearing my marshal badge, and who do I see but Happy Collins. He looked up and seen me at the same time. He smiled, and I smiled, and we threw our hands out and shook.

"Why Nat, you black son-of-a-shit-eating dog, how you been?"

"Better than you, I Have A Hand In My Ass, you horse-humping excuse for a white Indian."

We laughed and he invited me into the saloon for a drink, forgetting I wasn't exactly welcome inside. As a marshal, even a black one, I had some perks, but I didn't take advantage of them much, and besides, I didn't drink. I was still a sarsaparilla man.

"Someone has let you tote a badge?" he asked.

"Judge Parker don't care about color," I said.

"I mean why would they let you tote a badge. That's like asking me to be a banker."

It was all lame stuff, but we enjoyed it. Finally he went in the saloon, got a bottle of whisky and a bottle of sarsaparilla for me, and came out. We walked off to where there was a big oak on the edge of town, sat down there and talked while we sipped from our bottles.

"So what you been doing all this time?" I asked.

"These last three years were what you might call eventful," Happy said. "After Adobe Walls, I managed to brave up enough to go back to the Cheyenne. I mean, I waited until I heard they was near whipped in spirit, you know, and that White Shield, my father-in-law, had forgiven me. He had banished me because White Eagle said he should. Now on account of White Eagle being nothing but a lying asshole, he welcomed me back. You know, the Comanche and the Cheyenne gave White Eagle a new name after Adobe Walls. I ain't exactly sure how it shakes out, even though I speak both languages pretty good, but it's something like Wolf Pussy, or Coyote Ass, or Wolf Shit, Wolf Turd, maybe. Whatever it is, it's not meant as a term of endearment. He gets kicked a lot and women throw horse shit at him. I seen them do it. Thing was, though, even having been welcomed back into the fold, I didn't stay long. My wife, White Shield's daughter,

damn if she wasn't humping the hell out of a brave in
the short time I was gone. I think she had done him so
good he had gone cross-eyed. I sure didn't remember his
eyes being like that when I left out of there on the run.
Anyway, I got back into camp, I come to suspect it had
been going on all along and I had been a fool. I rolled
up my blankets and went back to white folks, and have
been miserable ever since. I liked being an Indian. You
know a thing I miss, though I don't say it too much? It's
boiled dog. I guess anyone can kill and skin and boil a
dog, but my woman could do it better than anyone I
ever knew. I've whacked a few pups on my own, skinned
them and boiled them, but it just isn't the same. Shit,
Nat. I ain't nothing but a lazy scoundrel and secret dog
boiler in white society. Out there among the Cheyenne
I was respected for not stooping to woman's work. Hey,
whatever happened to Jack?"

I told him.

"Oh damn, Nat. I didn't know."

"He was a brave one," I said.

"He was at that," Happy said. "I knew him and
knew of him for a long time. Lot of people hated him,
but there wasn't many didn't respect him. Or if they
they didn't, they didn't let on to his face."

He drank more of the bottle, and we talked for
awhile longer, until I realized all we had between us was
that day at Adobe Walls. I made excuses, one of which

was that it was best I not be seen with a drunk, and then I stood up and so did he.

While he was laughing at my joke about him being a drunk, I stuck out my hand, and we shook. He had tears in his eyes as we parted. I don't know if it was the whisky, or memory of that day, or if Happy was just the crying type.

⌇{ **13** }⌇

T WAS ANOTHER two years before I pulled off my badge and rode out to Adobe Walls. I still had Satan, and he was still one hell of a runner, but he couldn't run as long or as far as before. He had gotten old. But, in a short burst, there still wasn't a horse alive that could beat him.

Took the old trail out there, come to where I thought was about where me and Jack had found that dead man, scalped and cut up. There wasn't any more wild Indians about, least not in packs. The Comanche had all gone tame, or so it was said. I didn't see a single buffalo. It was if that hunter and the Comanche and the buffalo had never been.

When I came to Adobe Walls, I tied Satan off to a broken pole sticking out of one of the walls, and went inside where we'd had the fight. A lot of people had camped there. There was all manner of things thrown around, piles of shit here and there, where lazy assholes hadn't bothered to go outside. The roof was long gone. There was only the sky.

I stood at the window where Billy Dixon had made his shot. Over the years there was them that doubted it, and them that said he made it from the loft, but there wasn't any loft. And he didn't make that shot from the roof. I know. I was there and seen him shoot.

There was them among the Indians and the whites who said, yeah, he made that shot, but the Indian didn't die. He got hit in the elbow, or just got the breath knocked out of him by that long shot, and he lived. I doubt it. I seen him fall, and I have seen too many dead things drop; that shot killed him, I am certain.

Looking out the window at that rise near a mile away, I was overcome with emotion. Had Billy not taken that shot, them Comanche might have worried us down like a dog nipping at a wounded animal, worried us plumb to death. Thank goodness he took the shot. That shot had let them know White Shield's magic was no good.

But I hadn't really come out to see Adobe Walls. Oh, that was part of it, but there was more to it. I had ridden this way remembering those nights Millie and I had together. They hadn't meant that much to either of us in the long run, but we had been young and bold and I wondered now if she was a school marm. Not that I planned to look her up.

But even those memories of her wasn't why I had really come.

No.

It was Jack.

Shadows were growing long by the time I reached the wallow where the three of us had fought the Kiowa. Actually, the wallow had filled in a lot, mostly with grass. The grass was long and green there, and where Jack had fallen, not too far from it, there was a greater growth of grass, and there was blue bonnets and yellow flowers. The ground was rich there. Climbing off Satan's back I looked over that spot, turned my head and looked to where we had seen that trail of Indians traveling along, defeated not only that day, but forever. The prairie went on and on except where it was blocked by great rises of red and rust-colored rock. The sky, though beginning to darken, was so blue it near made me weep. Clouds tufted like cotton balls against it and there was a flock of birds racing across it. A light wind blew. I took in a deep breath. I felt as if I was taking in one of the last free breaths there would ever be.

I let go of Satan's bridle, because unlike in the past, he was now willing to stand and wait for me, having finally decided I was someone worth knowing and would supply him with grain. I strolled over to where Jack had fallen, got down on my hands and knees and plundered through the grass. I turned up bits of rawhide and finally a skull, or what was left of it. The top of it had been bashed in and where there should have been a left eye socket there was only a big hole that spread from socket to nose gap. There was smaller splits in the bone at the back of the skull—knife or hatchet strikes.

I prowled about some more, found more bones. Not many. Weather, animals and time had hauled the others away. I gathered up what I could, pushed down a swathe of grass with my foot and laid the bones on top of it. There was a small shovel in my gear. I got that and dug a hole that would hold all the bones. I put them in it and pushed the dirt back into the hole.

When that was done I stood up and tossed my head back and howled like a wolf. Why? I have no idea, but it sure felt good. I went back to Satan and pulled a short board I had brought out from a bag strapped across the side of his saddle. I had prepared it before coming. Carved into it, the carving filled with white paint, I had put:

BLACK HAT JACK.

HE DIED LIKE A MAN. RIGHT AFTER
THE SECOND BATTLE OF ADOBE WALLS.

I didn't have any dates on it, but I thought that better somehow. Besides, I had no idea when he was born, no hint of his age. Jack would have liked it simple.

I sat there until the shadows widened and the clouds was no longer visible, and there was only the stars and the moon.

I rode by moonlight back to Adobe Walls and camped there, in the store part with Satan in there with me. I took off his saddle and blanket and curried him and gave him grain. I hobbled him, though I felt he would be willing to stay with me now, even though the night.

There was some firewood and kindling someone had hauled in, and I used that to make a nice fire as the wind was turning chill. I had a cold dinner of jerky and water. I had chosen the store for the night because the idea of lying down in the saloon where I had been holed up against them Comanche didn't appeal to me. It was silly, but that's how I felt. Above me was only sky, and that made me feel less cramped. The walls about me cut the wind. I was glad of that and glad for my fire, as there was much wind that night. It came howling across the prairie and down from the high rocks and moaned all night.

When I awoke the sun was not yet up. The fire had died down, so I took a stick and stirred it up and put on more wood so I could boil coffee and bake biscuits in my little pan. They didn't bake too good because I was in a hurry. I ate and drank, put out my fire and saddled Satan.

I took my time. The wind was still now. The sky was starting to lighten.

I thought about riding back to where Jack had fallen, one last time. But I didn't. I knew it didn't matter. It mattered not at all. Me and Satan went north east.

{ AUTHOR'S NOTE }

T HE SECOND BATTLE of Adobe Walls really happened, though I have used the fiction writer's privilege of telling it my way. Bat Masterson was really there, as were a few of the other characters. And Billy Dixon did take that shot, and its effect on the Comanche is as I described. Many of the events mentioned happened, though as with most Western history, there are considerable conflicts as to who did what and when and who was there and who was not, and so on. You finally have to decide on what seems the most real and lie about the rest of it, which is the bread of butter of a story writer. I have done that freely.

Blacks in the west have been mostly ignored until late. They took part in many great historical events, and did much of the Indian fighting as part of the Ninth and Tenth cavalry. Racism kept their accomplishments under wraps until recently. I know nothing of a black man being at Adobe Walls, but they were at many Western events, and there sure could have been someone like Nat there. History for African-Americans is growing richer. For Nat's background I read slave and ex-slave narratives, and a considerable number of historical tomes, as well as the remembrances of those who had lived through those times and wrote about it.

As described in the story, African-Americans got a better shake out west, as the tradition there was more of a wait and see before deciding a person's worth. This was not always the case, of course, but it was preferred by many African-Americans to the slave states, and by many, to the northern states, which were not always comfortable for the dark of skin either. Many famous mountain men and deputy marshals for Judge Isaac Parker were black. One of the most famous deputy marshals was Bass Reeves. The list of accomplishments by people of color is long and varied. There isn't room for all of it here, but I hope you will be encouraged to find out more. It's there if you look for it.

Finally, though real historical characters are mentioned in this story, this is my version of events, and even the real characters are not meant to be represented in an exact and accurate manner. They have become mythology, and I have played with that mythology, attempting like all story tellers, and tall-tale advocates, to give them their own sweet myths.

A last note. Western language was colorful and varied. I have tried to capture it here, though I haven't made any attempt for it to be on the money, but Nat's use of was instead of were was common for many. Even now, listening to pure East Texas accents, I find them variable. Not just the sound of the voice but the use of the words.

My father was born in 1909, and memory of him, and stories he told me that were told to him, are very much alive here. Not any exact story, but the tradition of story telling, which when he was in the right mood to do, could be riveting. I also got the feeling when listening to him that I was hearing an authentic voice not much removed from the era he was talking about, stories passed down to him by kith and kin. I am keeping the tradition alive.

I should also add that though there have been two other stories about this character, and there will be a forthcoming novel, the time lines don't entire jibe. I wasn't sure what was what when I first start writing about Nat. I have also changed his speech patterns a bit for this novella and for that forthcoming novel.

As for history, I love it and care about it and have researched all manner of things, but as I said, I have not hesitated to shift certain things slightly when I felt it was in service of the story. Also, for those who are highly knowledgeable about guns, I want to thank you in the past for sending me a lot of contradicting, expert information. I should add that I appreciate your support, but if you feel that I have made an error here concerning any weapon or any piece of history, well, keep it to yourself.

Joe R. Lansdale
January 1, 2014